"She's a da[...] there, didn't she?"

"She never killed him," Johnny said.

"I read all about her. Belle Nelson. She also killed two Texas lawmen came to arrest her husband."

Slocum had all he could stand. "They were bounty hunters and they came for the wrong man."

The station man shook his head. "That's her story. You know that someone went back and shot that wounded one in the doc's office. I'd sure bet it was her done it. How many women her age could get the drop on a man like she did him? Some sheriff down there sent a letter to the *Cheyenne Leader,* and it said he was sure that her man was the outlaw they were after. Those two got kilt were law-abiding citizens of long record in his county and they died in the line of duty. Her man'd been on the run a long time."

"Don't listen to Lester too much. He's a troublemaker," Johnny said.

Slocum thanked him and checked on the prisoner lying flat on the roof. Strange she'd never mentioned the second man was gunned down in bed.

JAKE LOGAN

SLOCUM
AND THE
WIDOW'S RANGE WARS

JOVE BOOKS, NEW YORK

THE BERKLEY PUBLISHING GROUP
Published by the Penguin Group
Penguin Group (USA) Inc.
375 Hudson Street, New York, New York 10014, USA
Penguin Group (Canada), 90 Eglinton Avenue East, Suite 700, Toronto, Ontario M4P 2Y3, Canada
(a division of Pearson Penguin Canada Inc.)
Penguin Books Ltd., 80 Strand, London WC2R 0RL, England
Penguin Group Ireland, 25 St. Stephen's Green, Dublin 2, Ireland (a division of Penguin Books Ltd.)
Penguin Group (Australia), 250 Camberwell Road, Camberwell, Victoria 3124, Australia
(a division of Pearson Australia Group Pty. Ltd.)
Penguin Books India Pvt. Ltd., 11 Community Centre, Panchsheel Park, New Delhi—110 017, India
Penguin Group (NZ), 67 Apollo Drive, Rosedale, North Shore 0632, New Zealand
(a division of Pearson New Zealand Ltd.)
Penguin Books (South Africa) (Pty.) Ltd., 24 Sturdee Avenue, Rosebank, Johannesburg 2196,
South Africa

Penguin Books Ltd., Registered Offices: 80 Strand, London WC2R 0RL, England

This is a work of fiction. Names, characters, places, and incidents either are the product of the author's imagination or are used fictitiously, and any resemblance to actual persons, living or dead, business establishments, events, or locales is entirely coincidental.

SLOCUM AND THE WIDOW'S RANGE WARS

A Jove Book / published by arrangement with the author

PRINTING HISTORY
Jove edition / November 2007

Copyright © 2007 by The Berkley Publishing Group.
Cover illustration by Sergio Giovine.

ISBN: 978-0-515-14370-6

JOVE®
Jove Books are published by The Berkley Publishing Group,
a division of Penguin Group (USA) Inc.,
375 Hudson Street, New York, New York 10014.
JOVE is a registered trademark of Penguin Group (USA) Inc.
The "J" design is a trademark belonging to Penguin Group (USA) Inc.

PRINTED IN THE UNITED STATES OF AMERICA

10 9 8 7 6 5 4 3 2 1

Prologue

A meadowlark's shrill whistle cut through the early morning chill. Skirt in her hand, Belle hurried through the dew-damp grass for the outhouse, a weathered gray unpainted structure complete with its strong fecal odors wafting up as well as with spiders. She always dreaded spending any more time than necessary inside the small structure. Her plans for the day ahead filled her thoughts when she pulled the drawstring to open the door.

Bushy whiskers faced her with two dark eyes that bore the look of a rabid wolf. The man's tough calloused hands grasped her forearms and jerked her inside before she could shrink back. A scream trapped in her throat never managed to escape. Her heart thumping from fear, she gasped hard for air, her knees threatening to buckle. The man roughly slammed her back against the sidewall, and his fetid breath in her face smelled far worse than the contents underneath the bench seat.

"One peep out of you and I'll cut your throat." With one hand to steady her, he leaned out and closed the door. They were shut in the darkness, save for small beams of light that came through knotholes and cracks in the wood. Now she was alone with a madman who she'd never seen before. Cramps in her stomach threatened to bend her over.

"Who-who're you?"

He was standing on his toes with his back to her, peering out through a crack in the wall in the direction of the cabin. "You don't need to know."

"What do you want?"

He turned around, and she could see the frown of disbelief in his hard-set eyes. "We're here to get him."

"Who?" she asked, managing to straighten her dress in the front as she stood as far away from him as she could in the close quarters.

"Tray McGraw."

"Who?" There was no one there by that name.

"Quit acting so dumb, lady. That man of yours is who we're after."

"Hank, Hank Nelson. You think he's this McGraw?" A new fear rose behind her tongue. He was wrong—mistaken. Hank wasn't McGraw. Her face trembled when she shook it and she gasped for more air in the stinking closeness.

"There's a five-hundred-dollar reward on his head dead or alive—" The man went back to looking at the cabin through the slit in the wall.

"No. No, he's Hank Nelson. You're wrong."

"Lady, I know my business. He's McGraw."

She began to beat him on the back with her fists, screaming, "No! No, he's Nelson!"

His backhanded slap to her face made her see stars. "Shut up."

Her palm went to her burning cheek. She was shocked he would do such a thing to her. A slow realization crept in to her thoughts. This man would kill her for no reason. No reason at all. It made her knees weak. No coward, she still didn't want to die. Not in this foul-smelling outhouse, that was for sure.

Her gaze fell on the polished wooden grip of the six-gun in his holster. *Cock and shoot*. Nothing to it. Hank had shown her how to fire his—but in the outhouse, could she jerk it out and do that?

Any minute Hank would be bringing in the errant milk cow who'd run off in the night. Where was the rest of this gang? How many were there? Hank's own handgun was hung in his holster on a peg by the back door; she'd seen it there on her way out. He was unarmed!

She reached, grasped the gun's grip in her hand, and jerked it free. With her other palm, she cocked it and shot as the man whirled around. The explosion in the close confines made her ears scream as if there were hot needles in them. But worse than that, the man's rough hands clutched her throat and were pressing on her windpipe. She managed to cock the revolver again as he closed off all her wind. Then, with her strength fast fleeing, she jammed the muzzle in his gut and pulled the trigger.

The second blast was more muffled and threw him backward. The force tore his hands off her. His knees bucked into her. He shouted obscenities at her as he went down. Repulsed, she tried to draw herself away from him without any place to go.

Then, his weight against the door broke the small latch. He spilled half out of the crapper onto the ground holding his belly and moaning, "You gut-shot me! You gut-shot me! I'm dying!"

Die then. She stepped past him holding the gun ready in case he needed more. Away from her tormentor, she began to run for the rise the cabin sat upon. Hank would need his guns. Where were the others with the man? Hank had surely heard the shots. Her ears would never be the same, they still rang from the blasts.

At the back of the cabin she saw two men on horseback crossing the meadow firing rifles at something. Hank. That was the direction he'd gone in earlier to find Bessy. What could she do? Get the rifle down. Out of breath, she rushed into the cabin, put the pistol on the table. Standing on her toes, she took the Winchester off the wall pegs, then rushed outside using the lever to load the .44/40.

At the corner of the house, she used the log ends for a rest and fired at the rider on the black horse. He fell out of the saddle, and the one on the bay shot at her. She could see the puffs of smoke from his rifle. The bullets buzzed like hornets around her, some smacking into the side of the cabin. She didn't let up shooting at him until he turned and, beating his horse on the butt with his repeater, raced for the timber.

The heavy Winchester in one hand, her skirt in the other, she ducked through the rail fence and raced across the meadow. The black horse, dragging its reins, shied from her approach. Its rider was facedown and not moving. She ran past him, looking everywhere—then spotted the brindle milk cow.

Where was Hank? He had to be— Then she saw his boots in the grass. *Oh, dear God, let him live. Please.* She skidded on her knees to look in his face.

He forced a smile at her. "Sorry, Belle. Who were those fellars?"

Blood was soaking through his shirt and she ripped it open. The bullet holes were in his chest. The gravity of his wounds shocked her. She wet her lips searching for words. "Bounty—bounty hunters."

"You all right, Belle?"

"Yes—yes—I shot two of them." She scooted forward to cuddle his head in her lap.

"Who did they want . . ."

"Tray McGraw. I never heard of him. They thought you were him."

He barely shook his head. "Never heard of him."

She could see the pain written in his blue eyes and the life inching out of him. They didn't need to talk about trash like those three; these were the last minutes they would share on earth until the hereafter. A pain stabbed her in the chest as she bent over and kissed him. Kissed him and kissed him until she realized he had gone limp.

Tears began to spill down her cheeks. Hot tears that stung cascading off her face. She clutched Hank to her breasts and rocked him as if there was hope she could bring him back. Then she realized her bladder had let loose too. Oh, what else!

Then she heard something, and looked up in time to see the one she'd wounded struggling to get on his black horse. The animal acted spooked and the man had trouble getting it to stand, but he finally managed to get across the saddle and fought to get his right leg over the circling mount.

"No," escaped her lips. She set Hank down and ran for the rifle she'd dropped. Tripping over her hem sent her sprawling facedown in the knee-high grass. In desperation. she crawled on her stomach and elbows to the Winchester, and sent the last cartridges in the breech after the fleeing rider. With her eyes stinging from the black powder smoke, she last saw him, bent over in the saddle, obviously wounded. Horse and rider disappeared into the pines. In defeat, she buried her face in the sweet/sour-smelling timothy grass— the hay Hank had intended to start harvesting that week.

The funeral was the hard part, with all Hank's old friends and family for her to greet, accepting their teary-eyed condolences. In her black dress, she tried to stay stiff-backed and strong despite the hurting in her heart. Reverend Gipson, the small man behind the eyeglasses, was way too familiar. "Oh, my dear, I am so sorry. Hank was such a delightful person—I'm certain God in his wisdom has taken him to a better place."

Better place than being with her? She doubted that. With the Reverend patting her on the back, walking close like she needed support, and acting like they were old friends, it was about more than she could stand. She knew her looks attracted men, but Gipson was not the one she wanted. For the moment, she wanted no man except the two who'd shot Hank and she wanted them dead. As Gipson said at the graveside, "Vengeance is mine saith the Lord. . . ."

Vengeance would be hers when she got those other two in her gun sights. One of them was lying upstairs in Doc Green's office. The deputy said he wouldn't talk. When Hank's body was in the ground, she'd go up there and make him talk. He'd want to talk when she got through with him. She dabbed at her wet eyes and looked at the Wind River Range. Still snow in patches in the higher country. In two weeks she'd have everything sold, accounts settled, and be on her way.

". . . may he rest in peace. Amen."

"Belle, you're as welcome as can be to come to our place." Willy Stauffer's Adam's apple bobbed as he held his hat all wadded in his hands.

"Thanks to you and the missus for all your kindness," she said. "I'll be fine."

"There's talk you want to sell the N7 Bar?"

"Yes."

'Well, this ain't no place to talk business. I'm sorry."

"No, Willy. I'd sell the ranch and the cattle for four thousand dollars."

He looked at her hard. "That's lots of money, ma'am."

"Yes, but its got lots of irrigated bottomland. It has a good crop of timothy and in the other meadow alfalfa."

Willy nodded. "Hank was a good farmer for a Texan."

She knew the horse-trading game. Don't rush to drop your price. The buyer could hem and haw, make you think he was squeezing his chin because the price was more than he wanted to pay, when all the time he was stalling to see if the seller would break. Her father had taught her that when she was in her teens.

"Would you—"

Her head shake cut him off.

"Well, I sure hate to do business at a man's funeral with his—"

"Widow? I can meet you at the bank next Tuedsay in Riverton."

He squinted at her out of his left eye. "You're serious?"

"Willy, I'm as serious as I can be."

"Yes, ma'am. The bank in Riverton. At what time?"

"Make it at ten in the morning. I'll have the farm sale the next Saturday and you can take possession the following day."

"Would it bother you any if I sent the boys over to start cutting the hay?"

"Send them. I may not be there to cook for them."

He held up his hands in defense. "No, no. I never expected that. Can I ask you one more question?"

"Certainly."

"I know it ain't none of my business, but—are you going back to Texas to your family?"

She simply nodded.

"My dear Mrs. Nelson, would you come have lunch with all of us up at the schoolhouse?" the preacher asked. "The folks have prepared plenty to eat."

She noticed the sheriff was standing back and acting like he wanted to talk to her. "I'll be right along. Go ahead, Reverend Gipson."

"Oh, I know you must want a last minute alone with Hank. I could stay and pray with you."

She shook her head to dismiss him. When he started for the schoolhouse, the sheriff, Lewis Grimes, stepped over. A man of medium build, with graying hair and a white mustache, he swept off his white Stetson to talk to her.

"Mrs. Nelson, we're going to charge this galoot that's shot up with murdering your husband. When he gets to where he can travel, I'll take him to Riverton and put him in my jail until the judge comes for the court sessions."

"You don't know his name?"

Grimes shook his head. "He's tough, but he'll break down and tell us and we'll learn his other partner's name, the one that got away. The one that you—I mean, the one that was dead had a letter on him addressed to Jim Talbot, General Delivery, Burkhart, Texas."

"Maybe someone there knows them?"

"Yes. I'll send a letter to the sheriff down there. Is there anything I can do for you?"

"No—" She chewed on her lower lip, and then she raised her head to regain her composure. "Do you have any idea why they thought Hank was this outlaw McGraw?"

"No, ma'am, and no one I can find saw them ride into this country."

Her brows furrowed at the man's words. "No one saw them ride in?"

"No one. So they must have had someone and someplace to hide them. There's always a criminal element around that'll do any underhanded thing for money."

"Thank you, Sheriff Grimes. I appreciate all you're doing."

"Yes, ma'am," he said, and doffed his hat. "You're a brave woman for all you did. We can handle it from here on."

She nodded. *Or I will.* With her skirts in her hand, she headed for the whitewashed schoolhouse and the noisy children playing tag around the perimeter.

Inside the schoolhouse, crowded with folks that looked sad when they saw her, she spoke to the auctioneer, Taylor Nichols. A burly man with a rasping laugh and a drawl, he greeted her with his usual smile. "Why, certainly, Miss Nelson, I'll be proud to sell your things next *Sat-a-day*. But pardon me, ma'am, ain't it a little early for doing that?"

"No." She thanked him and started to move away.

He laughed out of obvious nervousness and nodded. "Guess you'd know better'n anyone when to have it. I'll be there with my help at daybreak on the day of the sale. And ma'am, thank you. I sure liked your man and this is a sad day in all our lives."

"Yes," she agreed, and went to look for Mathew. He was the gunsmith in town and Hank's close friend—she needed his advice. At last she saw him in the corner of the classroom talking to a rancher named Brothers. Mathew Gilliam was in his early forties, a widower, with enough gray on his temples to make him handsome. Of medium build, he still looked athletic, and walked straighter than most men, many of whom were cowboys.

"I'm going back to Texas," she explained to him. "I need a pistol."

He nodded as if in deep thought as they stood together. "No bigger than your hands are, I'd suggest a .32-caliber Colt. They're about two thirds the size of a .44."

"Sounds good. I want two and a holster for them."

Mathew looked at her in shock.

"Not here," she whispered in his ear. That cut off any words.

"I'll have them," he said under his breath, sounding uncertain about the whole matter.

"Excellent, I'll see you in the morning."

"Yes. . . ."

At eight the next morning, when he unlocked the front door of his shop, she came in dressed in a divided riding skirt and a man's shirt, with a felt hat on her shoulders caught at her throat by a rawhide cord.

"You're up early," Mathew remarked.

"Yes, Watson over at the blacksmith shop is shoeing two horses for me."

"Going back to Texas?" he asked, walking behind the glass case. Without a word he drew out a pistol and put it on the counter. "That's one of the .32s I have. Feel it. I'm not your father nor your keeper, but going off to Texas by yourself is not a wise thing to do even armed."

"I understand your concern, but we all have to do what we have to do."

"I know, Belle, but you can't run down cold-blooded killers. Why, land's sake, you're a woman."

She examined the revolver, making certain it was unloaded, then aimed it and squeezed off the trigger with a snap. It was much easier to handle than the heavier revolvers. "I'll take it and the other one."

"It's a little fancier." He shook his head. "It don't match that one."

"Get it out." She turned and watched a buggy go by. Her worst fear was that Grimes would move the wounded man before she talked to him.

Mathew set the walnut box on the counter. The silver-plated Colt had a mother-of-pearl handle. She leaned over and studied the firearm in the felt-lined box—not touching it. "How much? Bottom dollar."

"One-fifty, and I can't sell it any cheaper even to you, Belle."

"I'll take it. Where's the holster?" She removed the pistol from its case and hefted it. "Just right—cartridges?"

Looking upset, he set a box of .32 shells on the counter.

"The holsters?" she said, busy loading the copper cartridges in the side gate. "They'll need to be cut down."

The Colt loaded, she spun the cylinder around so the hammer was on the empty chamber, then set it on the countertop. She took the two-gun holster set from Mathew and strapped it around her waist.

"I can cut it down," he said, looking at the obviously too large fit.

"Do that. I'll be right back." She picked up the pearl-handled .32 and, with her gun hand close to her leg, headed for the door with him yelling after her.

"What are you doing?"

"Never mind, I'll be right back." She frowned with impatience at him and went out the front door.

Doc Green's office was half a block away. Grateful there were few people on the boardwalk, she nodded to Mrs. Ripple, who never noticed the pistol in her hand. At the foot of the stairs she looked around, saw nothing out of the ordinary, and took the stairs two at a time grateful the new hem cleared her boot toes.

The door was unlocked and she pushed inside the office. No one was there. Good. She slipped in to the hallway wondering which room held the man she wanted. With a hard swallow she took the pistol in her left hand and dried her right palm on the side of her skirt. Then, with the gun back in her right hand, she continued on tiptoe. A man's hard cough told her someone was in the next room on the left.

A tough-looking man blinked at the sight of her, then frowned in disbelief when she brought up the pistol.

"Who in the fuck're you?"

"I'm asking the questions here. I shot you once and will again unless you start talking—now, who are you?" She punctuated her threat by cocking the pointed gun at him.

"Lady, lady, put that gun down."

"Talk."

"You're going to hurt yourself—" His words were cut off by the shot she fired in to the pillow beside his head. Wide-eyed with fear, he bolted upright and held out his unbandaged arm to stop her in the smoky haze. "All right. My name's Turk Hayes. Go easy with that damn gun. Jim Talbot was the fella you killed. Wesley Harrigan was the fella got off. There."

Her eyes watered from the gun smoke and the smoldering pillow on the bed. But she had the names she wanted. "Whose place did you hide out at before you came to ours?"

"He might kill me."

"I can do that."

Hayes shook his head in defeat. "You know, you're one tough bitch. Olsen, Mars Olsen."

She turned and heard the man sigh in relief behind her back. At the doorway, she turned back to him, hearing the rush of feet coming up the stairs—her time would be short. "Where was Harrigan headed?"

He'd poured the water pitcher on the smoking pillow and now looked up at her. "To get the hell away from you, I guess."

The red-faced deputy broke in to the office, holding the rest back with his left arm, gun in his other hand. "Who's shot?"

"A pillow, I think," she said, and turned sideways for the startled crowd to make room for her passage down the staircase. They looked at her in silent disbelief as she went past them.

"It's all right folks. No one's shot," the deputy announced as she strode away down the boardwalk for the gun shop.

"You shoot him?" Mathew asked, looking around to see if anyone had trailed her to his store.

"No, only the pillow beside his head."

When she offered no more information, he laid out the adjusted holsters for her. She put the rig on and slid both guns into the holsters. After adjusting the buckle and settling it on her waist, she paid Mathew, who looked hard at her the whole time. He held the money she'd given him in his hand, still looking surprised. "I have one more gun you might need."

"Yes?"

"It'll fit in your boot."

She nodded, both pistols loaded and strapped around her waist.

He set a small handgun on the counter. "It's called a Ladysmith."

She nodded again, and he put two boxes of shells for it on the counter. "How much do I owe you?"

He waved her away. "My gift. I don't approve of your

goals, but I think you're the most beautiful woman in the world and I'd do anything for you. I have thought that ever since he brought you here."

"I never knew that," she said, looking the .22 over.

"Well, now you do. All those times I drove out to see Hank, well, it really was to catch sight of you." He stretched his arms over his head and covered a yawn. "Guess you know there ain't no fool like an old one."

"Mathew, I never considered you old nor foolish and I really think a lot of you. Thanks for the compliment. I'm flattered."

"Guess there ain't no talking you out of selling out and giving up on this crazy business of finding his killers?"

"I couldn't live out there. Too many reminders. Bad memories of that day would haunt me."

He agreed in defeat. "Belle, you ever need anything, I mean anything, let me know."

She reached over and pulled him against the counter. With a quick kiss to his cheek, she smiled at him. "I will, Mathew. I will."

A week later, she sat cross-legged on the ground in the predawn looking at the crude shack and the stinking pig-pens of a moonshiner named Olsen. Using a forked stick for a gun rest, she had both of her rifles loaded beside her. The first target she aimed to shoot at was a whiskey barrel on the bench beside the cabin doorway. Mars Olsen was going to get up early this morning.

The report of the rifle echoed across the hillside. She heard someone in the house begin cursing, and she aimed the next shot at the keg, which was already spouting out a stream of liquor from the first hole. A grizzly figure in gray long handles rushed out and bear-hugged the barrel to take it to safety. Her second well-placed bullet struck a stave and made the man drop the barrel on his toe. Then, with him yowling and hopping around on one leg with his foot in his hand, she splintered the door facing with another bullet close by his head.

Wide-eyed, he threw his hands in the air looking for her. "I give up."

"No," she shouted. "You get out of this country and don't come back. Forever."

"But my clothes—"

Her next bullet, near his foot, made a puff of dirt and he danced sideways, hands still high. "Get on that mule of yours and don't stop till you get out of Wyoming."

"I hear yah. I hear yah. I'm going." She put the rifle to her shoulder and sent another bullet in to the ground near his foot. After that, he really ran for the corral. Using a rope for a bridle, he bellied over the circling mule while whining and crying, "She's gonna kill me. Crazy gawdamn bitch. She's gonna kill me."

He rode off flailing his mule. With the smell of pigs in her nose, she recalled it was the same odor that had filled the outhouse that day. All the grunters soon were turned loose. She went to the cabin, found a can of kerosene, and spread it over the cabin's contents. At the doorway she struck a match on the door facing. When she tossed it on the coal oil, it went up with a whoosh.

Her rifles in the saddle boots, she swung up on the gray horse Hank had called Thunder and pulled on the lead to Sandy, the bay horse under the packsaddle. She looked back at the raging fire and nodded in approval. All she lacked was settling with Harrigan—it would be a long ride to Texas.

1

Cheyenne shone in the mid-afternoon sun. The railroad hub sprawled out to the fort. Another hot August day. Slocum sat on his haunches near the loading pens dickering over cattle prices with cattle buyer Hap Brehnam.

"They're all threes and fours?"

"I said that once, Hap. You can gate-cut any that ain't."

"I can't use them calves." Hap pushed the narrow-brim hat back on his head. "You say that they've got lots of Durham blood in them?"

"All mottled-faced or roans."

"How many head?"

"They drove two thousand up here, so taking an eight-percent death loss—say eighteen hundred."

"All steers?"

"Yes. They're damn good cattle. They've put on some good weight up here. Be big frames."

"All right, I can use them if they aren't—"

"Exactly like I said they were. We can take the train over to Rawlings in the morning and a stage north to the headquarters. You can see them for yourself. Let's go have a drink."

"Just what I need." Hap put his hat back on, refitted it to

suit himself, and rose. "How did you get hooked up with Butch and Tom Izzer on this deal?"

"I needed some work and they needed a manager."

"I mean, I remembered back in Dodge you made some drives; then after that, I didn't see you. Figured you cut out a place of your own when that good graze opened up north of Ogallala."

Slocum shook his head. "Guess I have itchy feet."

"There was some good-looking gal—what the hell was her name—Lucy VanDamm—had a bunch of cattle in the Cherokee Strip. You worked for her, I remember."

Slocum nodded as he recalled playing tag with her naked in a great high feather bed. Lucy VanDamm, there was lots of woman there. Him swatting her bare butt with his hand and her howling like he was killing her, until they both spilled apart laughing themselves into tears. Hard to forget a redheaded woman with that many freckles on her ass.

"She married a businessman from New York," Slocum said. "And sold out."

"Damn, I always figured she was hotter than a wildcat."

"She'd sure win that race all right." He paused to open the Longhorn Saloon's batwing door for Hap, and stared back at a woman riding a gray horse astride and leading a packhorse. Her looks were striking, and something in her eyes told him she was searching. Two guns strapped on her waist, a rifle under each fender skirt, this was no ordinary woman. The pistol in the holster on this side was silver-plated and had a mother-of-pearl handle.

"See something?" Hap asked.

He took one last look after her and then shook his head. "Nice gray horse."

They went to the bar, ordered a bottle and two glasses, then retired to a side table.

After two drinks, Slocum shook the man's hand and promised to meet him in the morning.

"Don't tangle with no wildcats," Hap said, and raised his third glass to him.

Curious about the gray horse's rider, he worked his way down Lincoln Boulevard looking over the horses in the various liveries. In Clancy's Finest Irish Stables, he spotted the gray in a tie stall with the bay. He walked down the alleyway, and a swamper came out chewing and spitting tobacco to help him.

"Whatcha need?"

"The gray? Who rode him in?"

"A fine lady did if it's any of your business."

Slocum reached in his pocket, took out a silver dollar, and flipped it in the air. "Heads you win, tails I kick the dogshit out of you for the answer."

"Heads. Her name's Belle Nelson and she's staying at the New York Hotel." He spat aside a large quid of tobacco and turned back holding his overall suspenders in both hands.

"Heads it is." Slocum tossed him the coin and he caught it with both hands.

"You want to leave a message?"

Slocum shook his head. Why did a fair-headed woman wearing guns and riding a gray horse have him so curious? Was it the verse in the Bible, in Revelations, about a stranger riding a gray horse? Striding back up the street, he looked in the plate-glass windows of each eatery until he saw her head in the lamplight. No mistaking her wheat-colored hair or the face—where had he seen her before? That was the attraction, he'd known her in another time—another place—but where? Then he was inside the café, looking around as if searching. Then he strode over with his hat in his hand.

"Ma'am, is this seat taken?" He indicated the chair opposite hers.

Her blue eyes searched around, as if looking to see how crowded the place was, and she saw seats available at other tables. When she looked back at him, her lashes narrowed and she lowered her voice. "You obviously want to talk to me."

"Yes, Belle."

"That voice. We've met before. Sit down." She nodded to the chair. Then, with her arms folded, she sat back to look him over. "Where?"

"I've been asking myself that for an hour. When I saw you come riding up Lincoln out there."

"How did you remember my name?"

"Honestly, I asked the swamper at Clancy's. But Nelson didn't fit."

She tossed her hair back. "How does Jarnagan work?"

"Justin Jarnagan—hmm, had a tomboy of a daughter could ride anything that breathed."

She made a face, looking uncomfortable. "He called me Butcher."

"Butch Jarnagan, you won the big stake race at San Antonio on a little mare I owned called Señorita. I owe her a plate of food."

"You made me so mad selling her after that race. I could of won a lot more on her."

He ordered coffee from the waitress, who brought Belle a plate of fried steak, potatoes, bread, and green beans.

"You can order food, I'm in no hurry," she said, indicating her portion.

"Fine, then you bring me the same thing," he said to the waitress. He turned back to Belle. "Your father?"

"Killed in a wagon wreck. Horses ran off. About six years ago."

"Well, your husband then?"

"Shot two weeks ago by some bounty hunters who thought he was an outlaw called Tray McGraw." She dropped her chin and shook her head. Then, using a napkin, she wiped her mouth as if to keep herself from crying. In the end she blotted her wet eyes with it.

"I did better than this—" Sniff. "At his funeral."

"We can talk about it later. Eat your food."

"I haven't eaten much in days. I realized I needed some strength and thought I could eat tonight."

"Eat. Where are you headed?"

"Texas."

"Why?"

"'Cause I shot one of the bounty hunters and wounded another. The sheriff's got him. He's going to hang for it. One got away. I figure he went back home. I'm going to find him and bring him back or bury him."

"What's his name?"

"Wesley Harrigan. You know him?"

He shook his head. "I've heard of him. He's a hired gun. He used to live in the Texas hill country. I heard he's been involved in some range wars."

"This wasn't a range war. They came to get my husband dead or alive as this Tray McGraw person. They shot him down unarmed."

"And you're setting out to take on one of the killers?" The waitress brought his food and he thanked her.

Busy sawing her steak with a knife in one hand and a fork in the other, Belle looked up at him and nodded. "Closer friends than you have tried to talk me out of it." She sawed some more and shook her head. "And you won't either."

He held up his hands. "I won't try. I have a week's worth of work left in Wyoming. I need to take a cattle buyer up to look at a herd, sell them, and then I'd be free to go along with you to Texas."

"Why would you do that?" She paused with a small triangle of brown beef on her fork.

"I owe you for all the money I made on that little mare." His steak must have come off the same critter, it was not tender. He took out his hunting knife and cut it in pieces. Then he handed the stag-horn-handled weapon to her. "This will be easier."

She used the big knife for a pointer and waved it at him. "If you think I am ever going to forgive you for selling her, I won't."

They both laughed and ate their food.

She finally broke the silence. "I'm not certain about your intentions, but I'd be a damn fool not to take you up on that offer. The farther I get away from there, the more I have decided the world is a damn sight bigger than a bride remembered it in getting there."

Slocum chuckled. "Ah, the honeymoon."

"I don't know if you ever knew Hank Nelson, but a woman could not have had a better husband. I had seven good years with that man."

Slocum nodded. "I've been up here in Wyoming since last year looking after these cattle for the Izzer brothers. I was going back south anyway. This just made leaving faster."

"What will I do—"

"Go along, no strings attached."

"My horses will be fine here. All right, now I've agreed to all your terms, what is your name?"

"Slocum, simple as that."

She let "Slocum" roll off her tongue, then she nodded. "I never thought I'd ever forget your name, I hated you so much for selling her."

"Maybe I'm halfway forgiven then?"

"Never."

He chuckled. She might be pretty, but there was something hard inside her. Maybe she'd forgive him someday— *surely.*

2

The train ride took eight hours, and Slocum, Belle, and Hap descended the car's steps after dark. Slocum hired a cab to the hotel, stopping by to be sure the stage for Landers left at six the next morning. They took supper in the Bellingham Hotel, and Hap, who had talked to Belle for most of the train ride, continued his conversation with her.

Slocum ordered Belle a room, and the pimple-faced clerk started to say something about not allowing single women to take hotel rooms. Slocum said softly, "You say one word about a single woman, I'll blow your tiny brain away."

He swallowed hard and nodded. "Yes, sir."

"That's better. We want to wake up at five tomorrow morning, not one minute later."

"That'll give us time to have breakfast," he said to his travel-weary companions. "There's a café down the street for workers that does a fine job of slinging hash. It'll be open."

"How long is the stage ride?" she asked.

"Twelve to fourteen hours. With no breakdowns." Or holdups. Wyoming had its share of both.

Slocum carried her carpetbag up to the room and unlocked the door. He looked around and set it down. "This suit you?"

She nodded and smiled. "Beats sleeping on the ground. Sorry I'm such baggage."

He never answered her apology and went on. "In the morning they'll wake us."

"I'll be ready. This man Hap must make big cattle deals."

Slocum agreed. "He's impressed with you."

"I'm not looking for a man, I want a killer."

"I understand. In the morning—" He touched his hat brim. "Sleep tight. May I suggest you prop a chair against the knob? It'll keep out the unwanted."

A serious look spread over her face and she nodded. "Thanks."

He strode down the hallway to his own room. Shame to waste two beds when one would have done fine for the two of them. With a smile on his face, he unlocked the door to his stuffy room, and went to the single window and opened the bottom half, looking down on Main Street. The night lights were being lit. Wagon traffic moved in the shadowy street. An engine whistle spooked some mules, and he could hear the driver cursing them and sawing on their bits for control.

Undressed and lying on the lumpy bed, he stared at the tin ceiling tiles in the room's darkness. It was hard not to think about Belle's voluptuous body under the man's shirt and the divided skirt. *Oh, what the hell. . . .* He finally closed his eyes and went to sleep.

At dawn, the three ate scrambled eggs, fried pork, and hot biscuits at the Three Square Café, then with their light luggage walked in the cool air to the stage office. Slocum saw a familiar figure standing on the porch. A tall, slightly bent man, Johnny Hewland looked up and shouted to Slocum.

"Slocum, you back so soon?"

"I ain't got enough of your wild driving yet. This is Johnny. That's Belle Nelson and Hap."

"Howdy, ma'am. You with him?" Johnny hung a thumb

at Slocum and took off his weathered and sweat-stained black hat for her with a bow.

"Yes. Sometime you must tell me all you know about him."

"It would take two books full to even start. Nice to have you going along, ma'am."

"I'll be waiting for the first book." She smiled at the man and his face grew a little red, as if looking at her was like sneaking an indecent peek at the woman under the clothing.

She patted his sleeve when she went by. "I see we have lots to talk about."

"Yes, ma'am. You three better get your seats, I'm hauling out of here directly." He opened the stage's door and Slocum used his arm to steady her ascent into the coach. Inside, he indicated the seat facing back. Hap sat across from them.

"Damn stage robbers." Johnny said, closing the half door. "I've been held up six times in the past three weeks. Better ditch your valuables. They're liable to hit us again."

No one else came out to ride on the stage, and Johnny, in his big coarse voice, took command up on the seat, calling out the names of the six horses. Slocum slouched down in his seat. With a nod for Belle, he pulled his hat over his eyes and planned to catch some sleep between there and the Sweetwater country, where he'd been headquartering the stock operation.

Rocking back and forth, they'd made one switch of teams, and were pulling a hard grade when the sound of Johnny cursing brought Slocum awake. The coach was halting, and Slocum put a hand out to stop Belle. "Don't go for your guns. Slip them off, leave them in the coach, and let them have what they can find. Your life's not worth that much."

Hap nodded and stripped off his holster. Slocum did likewise as a masked rider with a gun ordered them out.

"Men first, then her," he said as if she was no threat and he wanted the men out in case they tried to challenge him. Slocum came out, hands high, and stood by the wheel, and Hap joined him.

"Now you, lady," the robber said from behind the flour-sack mask, booting his horse in close.

"Drop the gun," she said in the coldest voice Slocum had ever heard.

Slocum blinked. The Ladysmith revolver in her hand was in the man's face. Obviously he'd turned to check on the men, and with the mask on was unable to see her bring the small gun up.

"I say drop it too." Johnny, in the box, had a sawed-off single-barrel shotgun pointed at the robber.

"Sumbitch," he swore, and let his gun hit the ground.

Slocum jerked him off the horse. Hap unmasked him and both men looked hard at their prisoner.

"You know him, Johnny?" Slocum asked as the driver climbed down from the top.

"Why, hell, yes, his name is C.V. Crammer. Used to work for the HT5 outfit. What the hell you doing holding up stages, boy?"

"You said it. Used to work for them. No jobs around here. I needed some money to get out of here."

Johnny looked at him critically, then shook his head. "He ain't the same one held me up at Sandy Point last week. How many of you are there?"

Crammer shrugged. "How the hell should I know? Some boys over at Atlantic City said it was easy if you done it right."

"Well, you sure enough had some bad teachers. Missy, you just earned yourself two hundred dollars. Wyoming Stage Lines is offering that reward for these birds."

"Load him on top and I'll tie him up," Slocum said. "He can ride up there till we get to Sweetwater and the sheriff can have him."

"His poor ole horse won't never make the run up there hitched in the back." Johnny shook his head at the sight of the horse's poor condition.

"Hap, unsaddle him and turn him loose," Slocum said, gathering some rope out of the boot. "Get up there, Crammer, and any tricks, Mrs. Nelson may shoot you anyway."

He gave her a wink as the grumbling ex-cowboy climbed up on top. Seated at last on his butt, he held his hands out for Slocum to tie them. Slocum shook his head. "On your belly. I ain't giving you a chance to get loose."

"Gawdamn—"

On his knees, Slocum gave him a shove. "Keep on cussing and I'll gag you. Savvy?"

Crammer's mouth shut, he nodded, and lay down on his stomach.

The saddle and bedroll were stowed. Belle and Hap were inside, and Slocum was on the seat beside Johnny when he waved the lines shouting, "Hea-yah, you lazy devils." They began to move north again up the hard grade. The horses were digging in and the stage was finally rolling.

"Lost all my momentum," Johnny said in disgust, and cracked his whip. The pull proved difficult. Hooves turned up dirt and rocks until at last the horses were in a long jog. In another hour the stage was at the next station and fresh horses were brought in.

The station man climbed up and looked at Crammer. He came down the side and nodded. "He's been hanging around here for a week. I ain't surprised he was one of them."

"He's out of work," Slocum said before drinking from a dipper gourd out of the water pail.

"Hell, who ain't out of work?" the station man said, watching Belle go by and get in the coach. Under his breath, he said through his teeth, "I'd sure fuck her, but—"

"But what?"

"I figure she's a damn black widder. She killed her husband up there, didn't she?"

"She never killed him," Johnny said.

"I read all about her. Belle Nelson. She also killed two Texas lawmen came to arrest her husband."

Slocum had all he could stand. "They were bounty hunters and they came after the wrong man."

The station man shook his head and checked to be certain she couldn't hear before he went on in a low voice. "That's her story. You know that someone went back and shot that wounded one in the doc's office. I'd sure bet it was her done it. How many women her age could get the drop on a man like she did him? Some sheriff down there sent a letter to the *Cheyenne Leader,* and it said he was sure that her man was the outlaw they were after. Those two got kilt were law-abiding citizens of long record in his county and they died in the line of duty. Her man'd been on the run for a long time."

"We got to roll," Johnny said, and motioned for Slocum to get up on the seat.

"Don't listen to Lester too much. He's a troublemaker," Johnny said through his teeth while undoing the lines from the brake handle. He stomped the brake keeper pedal off and shouted. They were northbound.

Slocum thanked him and checked on the prisoner still lying flat on the roof. Strange she'd never mentioned the second man was gunned down in bed.

3

Crammer was bound over to the sheriff and stuck in the Sweetwater jail. Slocum rented a four-seated buckboard with a fringed top and the best spanking team Joe Darby owned. Their luggage on, he set out for the headquarters in the late afternoon. With Belle beside him and Hap in the back row, they left town in a hurry. Wind swept the sagebrush-covered land, and the dusty road followed the rustling cottonwoods along the river. A fan of brown tailed them as he fast-trotted the stout horses.

"See that bunch of steers on the rise?" Slocum said, pointing them out to Belle.

"Yes, they have lots of Durham blood in them," she replied.

Slocum shook his head, then winked privately at her. "I've been telling Hap that since before we left Cheyenne."

She agreed with a grin.

They drove past many more bunches of speckled or mottled-faced cattle spread out across the land. The fiery sun began to sink, and Slocum knew they'd not make headquarters before dark. He apologized to them, and drove on in the twilight until the lamps of the headquarters across the valley twinkled in the fading light.

"Supper isn't too far away," he promised.

The Mexican cook, Vasquez, looked the most pleased to see them, and he pumped Hap's hand when Slocum introduced him.

"Señor, I am so glad to see you. Now I can go home."

"Where's home?" Hap asked the man.

"San Antonio, where it don't snow."

The ranch hands laughed at his words and all of them took off their hats for Belle.

After supper, Slocum gave her his room to sleep in. She told him it wasn't necessary, but she accepted it. He and Hap took bunks with the hands.

"I'll ride out and look at some more of these cattle tomorrow," Hap said, struggling to pull off his boots. "That's what they pay me for. Guess you're anxious to go find her husband's killer?"

"I reckon," Slocum said, and climbed in the upper bunk. "Her father was a good man. He showed me lots about horse racing I never knew. I owe him that much."

"Horse racing? You've been working cattle, driving herds the last few years."

"They're the only paying jobs between here and the gulf."

"It ain't the best of times. Them rich fellas can sure mess up the economics and money business back there in New York."

"I don't know who does it, but you can have a deal made and it falls apart two weeks later. Night, Hap." Slocum pulled up the covers.

"Night."

For a long while, Slocum looked at the underside of the shingle roof in the faint light from the one candle on the table in the center of the room. The air reeked of dirty socks, tobacco, and sweaty saddles, and there were the snores of half a dozen hands.

What was Belle like? He'd been around her several days

and felt he knew little more than that she was agreeable and damn good-looking. Maybe the future would tell him more. He rolled over and went to sleep.

At dawn, Vasquez beat on a triangle and woke Slocum. The grumbling crew got up, washed their faces, dressed, and headed for the cook shack. They lined up, getting their tin cups of coffee and metal plates full of food, then took places at the benches. Slocum saw Belle was already at the head table, looking fresh.

He set his food down and smiled. "Sleep well?"

"Oh, yes, it was good to get out of those coaches."

"I was still moving myself." He looked around for Hap, spotted him, then stepped over the bench to sit beside her. "We'll be a few days settling this cattle business. Then we can ride on."

With a small smile, she nodded. "I understood you had business to attend to out here."

A short cowboy with a salt-and-pepper handlebar mustache stood across the table holding his hat.

"This is Neal Guthrie, my foreman," said Slocum.

"Nice to meetcha, ma'am. The boys been wondering when this job was over. . . ."

Slocum indicated the bench opposite. "Neal, I think Hap'll take the cattle. Roundup and drive and all, we've got a month to six weeks worth of work. The Izzer brothers want the wagon, mules, and gear took back to Texas. Vasquez can drive it. The ones want to drive the horses can go back with him."

"That's good news." Neal nodded with a look of relief. "Getting stuck up here ain't anyone's desire today. There's lots of out-of-work hands around."

"That's what they made Texas for—these fellas," Slocum said, and laughed. "Morning, Hap, you ready to ride today?"

"Yes."

"Neal, show him the cattle."

"All of them?" Neal grinned at the buyer.

"All of them," Slocum said, and shared a look with Belle.

The hands, all smiling over the news about going home, rode out in pairs to check the perimeters of the range and drive in the wanderers. Neal and Hap left in a long trot for the west. Slocum blew the steam off his coffee.

"Neal can make the cattle drive to Cheyenne. When the sale is sewed up, I can leave," he said, looking off at the distant mountains.

"You don't have to deliver them?"

He shook his head. "I'm kind of like Vasquez. I don't want to spend another winter in the snow either."

"It is different up here than it is in south Texas," she said softly.

He glanced over at her. "You regretting all this business?"

With a toss of her wheat-colored hair, she looked at him with a hard set in her blue eyes. "I'm impatient to find my husband's killer."

"I understand." He glanced away, after seeing the turmoil churning inside her in search of revenge—some sort of retribution for what the killer had done to her.

"I'm grateful you agreed to help me. But I worry I have been distracted too much coming out here while the killer is free—"

Slocum turned and clapped his left hand on her shoulder. "We'll find him."

She dropped her gaze to her boot toes. "I know. I need to rein in my impatience."

"I need to write a letter to my boss, so I'll need my room for a short while."

"No problem. Vasquez likes my help. I'll go and assist him."

"You must've got up early?" he said, realizing she'd helped make breakfast.

"No problem."

"You're a guest here."

"Working doesn't hurt me."

"I wasn't worrying about you. I was worrying how it might spoil Vasquez."

They both laughed and parted.

> *Dear Butch and Tom,*
>
> *Your move to winter the herd up here looks like it will work out as profitable as you two planned. The cattle will be driven to Rawlings in a week, weighed, and loaded on cars there. Arrangements will be made to transfer the money from the sale to your bank in Austin. Since I am leaving this week, I will have all the arrangements made. Neal Guthrie will be in charge. I have known this buyer Hap Brehnam for several years and he is reputable.*
>
> *Neal and Vasquez will bring the things you specified back to Texas as well as the cowboys that want to go along. I included them since there is not any employment in Wyoming for them and they have been hardworking and loyal.*
>
> *We discussed early on, in the event I needed to leave here for personal reasons, that I would turn things over to Neal. So since this deal is about to close down successfully and I have some pressing personal business elsewhere at this time, I'll put him in charge.*
>
> *After the sale is completed, Neal will telegraph you the details.*
>
> *Been nice working for you. I'll drop by Austin later and settle up with you two.*
>
> *Slocum*

He put the letter in an envelope, sealed it, and addressed it to them. He'd mail it when he and Belle got to Rawlings.

Texas. He would soon be headed back there, and in the company of an attractive woman. He rubbed the whisker bristles around his mouth with his fingertips. A bath and shave might not hurt. He took his change of clothes and towel to where the sheep-herder showers were set up. Three water barrels were set up head high on a rack and warmed by the sun. A rope hung down from under each one, and pulling on it let the water loose to shower down on the bather. Release it, and it sprang the spigot shut until a user needed more.

He was naked, and the wind swept his skin and made him think twice about doing this so early in the day. He took a deep breath, and the first shower of water felt like ice. Wet, he released the rope and began to lather up.

"Is it warm?" Belle asked.

He started at her words and whirled around. "No!"

She smiled, unbuttoning her shirt. "Go on. I'm not looking. But thanks, Vasquez said I could use one of those showers."

With his back to her while he soaped up, he laughed. "Hell, you didn't need his permission."

"I thought I better ask."

He started to turn around, and then thought better of it. Might have been nice to see her in the buff, but that too could wait. Finished lathering himself, he took in his breath for the rinse. Whew!

Her scream forced him to turn. Water was pouring over her head and her body, her pear-shaped breasts dancing to the high knee movements of her snowy legs. "It's really c-cold."

"Too cold," he agreed, turning his back to her and reaching for his towel. She looked even better undressed than he'd thought.

"Oh," she said, sounding shivering cold. "I was looking

for a warm bath. This is like wintertime. Oh, my. Vasquez said the sun warmed it."

"Usually does. The boys must have refilled it last night. That's straight from the windmill." He hung the towel on the peg and began to dress.

"You didn't mind me being so bold?"

He shot a glance at her bent over under a coating of white foam. Was she testing him?

"No."

"I thought I'd better do this while the hands were out working."

"Fine."

"You have no wife? Family?"

"No one but me." He pulled on his canvas pants and put up his galluses.

"I see."

She pulled the rope and screamed under the splash of the shower. He picked up the flour-sack towel and stood outside the ring of slatted boards. When he held the towel out to dry her, she blinked, then nodded and twisted away for him to start on her back.

Wrapping her arms around herself, she trembled with the cold as he wiped her back dry and studied her shapely bare butt. Her long thighs led to two shapely legs, and her bare feet shuffled to try and gain some warmth. When she turned, she took the towel from him and covered her breasts.

"I think I am getting over you selling that mare."

"No big deal, and it happened a long time ago."

"You forgot. I never did."

"Shame we've missed so much fun over that."

She shook her head. "No, I had my husband picked out even then. He was what every Texas ranch girl wanted. Blue eyed, blond, handsome. A man's man. He could rope or ride better than anyone I knew."

"Shame you lost him."

"Worse than that. They took him from me."

He nodded and started for his socks and boots. "You know killing him won't bring your husband back either."

"I know. I know. But I'll know I did all I could."

"Yes, ma'am."

"If you don't approve of me killing him, why are you going with me?"

"Kind of a debt. I owed your pappy for all the things he did for me. Plus I owe you for selling the mare." Socks on, he pulled on his boots and tried not to look over at her.

"Yes, you sure do." She shook her head and buttoned up. The pin-striped shirt covered all but the pink bottoms of her butt. Lots of woman there, and she aroused him. More than he let on to her. He thought of the image of her riding up Lincoln Avenue on the gray horse and coming into his life—them getting together must be in life's plans. *He'd see.*

4

They left Rawlings on the 3:18 for Cheyenne. The *chug-chug* of the engine starting out soon became the *clack, clack* of the rails under the passenger car wheels as they sped at twenty-five miles an hour eastward. With the cattle deal closed with Hap and the roundup under way at the headquarters, he'd left the rest for Neal to deal with.

"We'll be in Cheyenne past noon tomorrow," Belle said.

Now dressed in his suit, Slocum set down the newspaper he held in both hands. "Yes, I think that's the schedule. You glad to be back on track?"

"Yes. May I lean on you?"

"Of course."

"I didn't want to embarrass you."

He lowered his voice. "It might go smoother anyway if we acted as husband and wife from here on."

"Mrs. Slocum?"

He shook his head. "Mrs. Tom White."

"Why, Tom, darling," she drawled, and fiddled with his lapel. "I think that would be wonderful."

He did too. They both laughed.

In Cheyenne the next day, they registered as the Whites in the Place Hotel. Slocum went to see about a saddle horse and another packhorse, plus some camping gear. He returned to their room close to supper time, and she stood up to greet him wearing a blue dress.

"That looks nice," he said, setting his hat down on the bureau and admiring her.

"I didn't want to embarrass my husband." She walked over and embraced him. With her cheek on his shoulder, he rocked her back and forth. "At times I get so upset thinking about how this turned out. Not about you, no, you're an angel. I mean my life—I had everything I ever wanted—then they ruined it. Hold me and I'll try not to cry.

"Oh—" She sniffed. "There was this preacher back where I grew up. Stupid little man who was supposed to be comforting me, I think, and tried to rape me."

"I'm sorry."

"Guess I've been on edge around men ever since."

Her light lilac perfume wafting up his nose, he raised her chin with the side of his hand and kissed her softly on the mouth. Her palms slid over his suit and around his neck. They kissed harder, until they came apart and tried to catch their breath.

"We better go eat," he said, and turned her toward the door.

With half-closed eyes, she smiled up at him. "Why, Tom, do you think I'd never let you out of this room if we dillydallied for very long?"

"No, I'd keep you here till hell froze over." He opened the door.

"Sounds interesting."

He swatted her fanny with his palm and sent her out into the hall. "It will be."

They walked to the Peacock Restaurant in the last rays of sundown. The maitre d' showed them to a secluded table and gave them menus in fancy script. The flickering lights danced on her frowning face. Slocum grinned at her. "You can't read it. Every bit's in French."

Amused, she put it down as a waiter filled their glasses with water and promised them Rogain, the restaurant's owner, would be right there.

"So what do we eat?" she asked Slocum.

"Whatever Rogain says is good."

"Fine." She folded her hands on the table and made a knowing face at him. "How long will it take?"

"The meal?"

"Yes."

He reached over and squeezed her hands. "I'm not certain. But I'll make certain they hurry."

"Good," she said in a whisper as Rogain arrived in his tuxedo.

"Ah, Monsieur. What may I do for you and the lovely lady?"

"You have some slow-cooked lamb ready?"

"Indeed we do."

"Bring us a rack of that, some red wine, and some of your sourdough bread and butter."

"Wonderful. Coming right up." The man acted as if he understood their haste and left them.

She wet her lower lip with the tip of her tongue. "I'll try to show some restraint."

"Not too much."

After the mouth-watering, smoky-tasting, tender ribs became a pile of white bones, and the crusty bread and butter were nearly gone, they toasted each other with the last of the wine. He paid Rogain and they slipped out on the street. Under the streetlight he spotted the two riders and the blanket-butt Appaloosa coming up their way, and gently pushed her in to the dark doorway and kissed her.

"My, my," she said. "You are excited."

"I have some problems. They just rode by. Get our things from the hotel room and meet me in the alley. Here's the money to pay the clerk. Say we've been called away by a death."

"What'll you do?"

"Get the horses and things I have for us to take along and meet you in the alley in less than an hour."

"Who are they?" she hissed.

"Abbott brothers from Kansas. Deputy sheriffs. It's a long story. I can tell you going back."

He pulled her to him and kissed her. "Any questions?"

"No, but you aren't getting away, remember?"

"Yes, ma'am."

An hour later, they crossed the tracks and headed south in a long trot under the stars. With two packhorses in tow, Belle was on the gray and he was riding the big bay he'd bought. At dawn they found water in a creek, hobbled the horses away from the main road, and ate some jerky to keep from building a fire. Seated on his spread-out bedroll, he wished the Abbott brothers in hell for the twentieth time since he'd seen them in Cheyenne and they'd ruined his special evening with her.

"Why are they after you?"

"Years ago, a young man lost some money at cards. He was too drunk to really play, but he insisted. So when he lost, he got belligerent, accused me of cheating, and went for a gun. He ended up dead. His family is very prominent there and his grandfather has lots of money. I left Fort Scott and he's sicced those two brothers after me ever since then."

"But justice—self-defense?"

He shook his head. "They own the judge and jury."

"How did you know it was them in Cheyenne?"

"Louis always rides that Ap horse with the moon spots on his blanket."

She looked at the azure sky over them for help. Then, on her knees, she scooted over to him and looked in his face. "They can't find us here for a while, can they?"

With a grin, he shook his head. "This ain't a feather bed."

"Well, no feather bed," she said, then wrinkled her nose, spilled down on the bedroll, and began pulling off her boots.

He rose and toed his own boots off. Then he undid his gun belt and took off his hat, suit coat, pants, and shirt. When he turned, she was under the top blanket and had pulled it up to cover her breasts.

"No shame at all," she said, shaking her head at him, and held the blanket up for him to join her.

He slipped in, lay down beside her, then rolled over and kissed her mouth. His left hand molded her pear-shaped breast. She pulled him to her with a maddening hug. Her hot tongue slipped past his teeth and sought his mouth. Eager fingers began groping at the rock-hard muscle cords across his belly, then soon combed his stiff public hair, and her palm began stroking the half-hard erection as she inched over toward him.

His hand slipped between her parted legs, and he rubbed the crease until she raised her butt off the bedroll and thrust it at him. Then his finger sought her ring. Under his index finger's teasing, her clit rose and she began to moan in the arms of passion.

Wild with his needs, he eased himself on top of her, fitting between her silky legs. Her breathing was hard and fast, and she squirmed with an urgency to have him. Every nerve ending in his erection pleaded to be inside her. His butt filled with the need to pump his hard shaft into her. His entry drew a sharp cry and she clutched him tight.

On a storm-tossed sea, they fought the battle for finality. His rise and fall was like high waves slapping the side of a boat. Their pubic bones smashed tight, grinding the coarse hair between them. Her back arched thrusting her against him each time. Then, from the depths came the warning cramp and he pressed hard and deep inside her. Her legs, wrapped around him, tightened in preparation for the explosion that filled her.

Then she slipped off into a faint and her eyelids closed. He braced himself above her and smiled. Finally, she half-opened them and grinned at him. "Thank you."

"My pleasure."

"I didn't know how much I missed doing it—it's been over three weeks."

"Long enough. But we better head for Texas if we're ever going to get there."

"The superintendent and the hussy," she said, and laughed as he straightened.

"I'm sure not the superintendent anymore, and I certainly won't call you a hussy."

"I guess there's some guilt in my mind. Him not cold in his grave and I'm making love to you." She reached over, picked her shirt up, and started to put her arms into it.

"You don't need to have any guilt. We aren't hurting anyone." He glanced down at the pear-shaped breasts before they disappeared. She was sure some woman; it was a shame that misinformed bounty hunters had destroyed her life. He dressed and then loaded the horses. They had dry cheese and crackers, with a promise to each other to have better food at their next encampment.

In the next few days, they swung east to avoid Denver, moving southward. He was anxious not to leave a trail for the Abbott brothers. So in a week they were descending off the Sangre de Cristos into New Mexico.

"We need to get the shoes reset on our saddle horses," he said, viewing the low set of buildings. She nodded as they sat in the saddle stirrup to stirrup, looking through the heat waves at the village.

"You know this place?" she asked.

"Campo. I know a man who lives near here, or he did. I'm sure we can stay with him if he still lives here."

"Does he have water enough for a bath?"

Slocum laughed. "Oh, you want a bath?"

With a quick nod of her head, she smiled. "Yes."

"Well. Lets see if Campo del Norte has enough water for that."

"There are times you tease me and I am never certain what you really mean."

He reached over and patted her leg. "There will be a place to bathe there."

"Good." She checked the impatient gray. "It might take a hard soaking to get me clean."

He agreed and they moved out.

Curs rushed out to bark at them. Several Mexican women looked at them, while hanging wash or working under a ramada, to see who had arrived. Near-naked brown children with dark eyes left their games and in silence lined up to see the two pass by. Slocum reined up at the cantina, dismounted, and handed her the reins.

"I'll see if my friend still lives near here."

The cantina was empty at midday save for the short Mexican bartender. "Ah, Señor. What will you have?"

"I look for an amigo. Don Jeminez. He still live around here?"

"Ah, he lives at Rancho de Vaca."

"How far is that?"

"East about *quatro kilómetros*." He pointed to the back of the bar.

"Is it hard to find?"

"No, you follow the road and you will find it."

The man smiled, made a swipe with a rag at the polished bar top. "Where do you know that old mule rider from?"

"Buffalo hunting ten years ago."

"Yes, he hunted many seasons till they were gone."

"He rode a mule back then too," Slocum said, thanked the man, and left.

"We're close," he told Belle. "He lives four miles or so east." He mounted and noticed the five horses at the hitch rack in front of the general store.

"They came in while you were inside. They're not cowboys," she said under her breath with a frown. "More like hired guns."

Slocum nodded. Then he spotted the one standing guard on the front porch, cradling a Winchester in his arms. Not a good sign. They were either being cautious or up to no good. He dismounted and shook his head at her not to say a word. Keeping an eye on the storefront, he fumbled with his latigos until four men came out laughing and talking with lots of bravado in their voices.

None were familiar and the leader, with a red silk kerchief tied around his neck, saw Belle, took off his hat, and bowed. "My honor, madam *moiselle*."

She gave him a short nod and checked the gray.

"Ah, I see you have a husband. Ah, it is my bad fortune. But you are a most beautiful lady. Let's ride. Good day." He vaulted into the saddle to show off and waved to her as they galloped away.

"Who were they?" she asked.

Slocum swung in the saddle. "Just who you thought they were. Hard cases. But why have hired guns in this country?"

"I don't know."

"They weren't passing through either."

"What now?"

"Go see my old buffalo hunting amigo."

"You have never been to his place?"

Slocum shook his head, still concerned about the presence of the five gunmen. They were being extremely cautious. Leaving a guard with a rifle outside while they went in a store meant they expected trouble in the sleepy town. Something was astir.

"Don Jeminez and his wife Juanita used to live on a small ranch south of Las Vegas. Last time I saw them down there, she had just inherited a rancheria and they planned to move up here."

"Is it a large one?"

"Large enough for several families. These ranches were set up more like community cooperatives. The owners live in the village and they have so many livestock permits on the commonly owned range. It began a long time ago under the Spanish when, because of the Comanche and Apache, they needed communal protection to live out here."

"So it's a lot different than what we do, say, ranching in Texas."

"Yes, there's many different ways with the Mexican people in the region. The king of Spain even gave their ancestors this land."

"I'm anxious to meet your friends."

"But more anxious to get a bath." They both laughed and Slocum wondered, riding across the vast land covered with brown short grass, what those five hard cases were doing out there. *Up to no good—probably.*

5

Rancho de Vaca sat on a knoll under some cottonwoods that had been planted long ago and that rustled in the afternoon wind. A series of small irrigated fields were set below the hillside. Many were green with alfalfa, and half-dead corn plants with long ears drooped down. Rows of well-weeded frijoles, black beans, and peppers lined others. Boys in their teens from under straw hats looked up from their hoeing at Slocum and Belle and waved.

Slocum and Belle rode across the hollow-sounding plank bridge. In the small ditch underneath it, the turbulent irrigation water rushed to water some crop down along the ditch system. The exterior fortress wall that surrounded the place remained, but the tall gates had long ago been removed and used elsewhere. He led the way through the narrow passage to the open square, and dismounted to water their thirsty animals.

"Where do Don Jeminez and Juanita live?" he asked the woman busy washing below the pump.

"You are here to see them?"

"Yes, we are old amigos."

The woman nodded to Belle, who had dismounted and removed her hat. "Tia, go run up and tell Juanita she has company down here," the woman said to a young girl of perhaps twelve wearing a thin, flowered dress that hardly fit her.

Her bare feet took her away before Slocum could even stop her. "Juanita might be busy," he said.

The woman, back at her washing, shook her head. "One is never too busy in this village for company." Then she laughed. "So few ever come, we usually celebrate even a second cousin coming by."

Slocum undid the girths on the four horses. "They still call this place Rancho de Vaca?"

"Yes, a very important name, huh? Place of the Cow."

"Doesn't everyone have cattle here?"

"Some have sheep too. But things are bad here."

"Bad here? I don't understand?"

The woman looked up at the sight of another woman and the girl coming at a run and nodded. "Juanita can tell you all about it."

"Slocum! I never expected you. And who is this lady?" Juanita stood five-six, tall for a Mexican woman. Her slightly curled black hair carried some threads of gray, but she stood straight-backed and her beauty radiated despite her age. "I can't wait until my husband sees you. He will be so excited."

They hugged, and Slocum introduced Belle.

"Oh, Señora, I am so glad to met you." And they hugged.

"Some men mistook her husband for an outlaw and killed him," Slocum said. "We are on our way to Texas looking for one of those men."

"Oh," Juanita said, and put her arm around Belle's shoulder. "Come with me. Slocum, bring the horses. My husband will be so excited to see you both."

"Can we have a fandango tonight?" the washerwoman shouted after her.

Juanita stopped and looked at Belle. "What do you think?"

"Sure." Belle shrugged.

"*Sí.* Pass the word." When she turned back to Belle, Juanita said, "You will have a good time. Mexican people always have good times."

"I'll look forward to it."

The horses were put up and fed some hay, and Slocum rested in a hammock under the ramada while inside the women were busy bathing. Sounding like magpies, they laughed and talked as he rested his eyes. Grateful for the reprieve from being in the saddle all day, he felt the Abbott brothers had lost his track again. But the ranny with the red bandanna in town bothered him—he knew him from somewhere else and his gut feelings weren't good. He fell asleep.

"Your turn to bathe," Juanita said, waking him. "The water is hot. Toss out those clothes. We'll wash them while you clean up. There is a robe you can wear while they dry."

"Yes, ma'am," he said and swung his legs over the edge. Mopping his whisker-grizzled face with his palms, he combed his hair back with his fingers. "It's good to see you again."

"Oh, yes, and my husband will be so glad to see you. Now get going, we have things to cook for tonight and work to do."

"He's out checking cattle?"

"Yes. I expect him to be home by dark."

"Why do you sound so hard when you talk about him?" Slocum looked her in the eye. Something was wrong here.

She wiped her upper lip on the back of her fist. "I worry much for him. The Texas ranchers have pushed many cattle on our land like they own it."

"I wondered why we saw these five rannies in town."

"Killers—they have shot several of our people in the back."

"And your husband?"

"I worry every day he rides out that they will kill him."

"I understand—" He rose and stretched his arms over his head. "I'll get my bath and get out of your way." He winked at Belle as she came out on the porch brushing her hair. "You two make quite a bossy team."

Belle pretended to hit him with the hairbrush when he went by. "You'll see bossy."

After his bath, he put on the robe and met Belle in the doorway. She was holding a sheet over one arm and some scissors in her other hand. "You need a haircut."

He ran his hand over the back of his head. "I do. I guess you give shaves too?"

"For a price."

"I am a poor man." He turned his palms up at her.

"We'll see later how poor you are. Get out there on the stool."

"My, my, why did I bring you here? You've not been here a half hour and you have taken on Juanita's ways."

Belle swung the sheet around him and tied it at the back of his neck. "I like her," she said softly in his ear.

The snip of the blades and the locks of her cuttings dropping on his shoulders and chest made him realize how long his hair had become. Good, he would be cooler too. He winked at her when she looked at her work. She gave him a scowl and went back to snipping. "You may hate me after this."

"Not likely."

"Juanita sounds concerned about the Texans," she said.

"I need to learn more about them."

"What can you do? Get yourself killed?" She frowned her thin brows at him.

"I don't plan on letting that happen."

"Good, I would be upset."

He patted her leg as she reached over him to cut some more.

She stopped, closed the scissors, and looked hard at him. "Careful, I might make a mistake."

"I doubt that."

They both laughed and she went off to borrow a razor, brush, and soap from Juanita. He studied the small village. Brown children at play with sleepy burros. Women with their washing in baskets on top of their heads. Others using yokes to carry water in buckets. The place was like an anthill of activities. Gentle people who loved the land and each other. Not many conveniences here that one found in cities, but the people here probably never knew about them and wanted to stay here on their land.

She returned and began to soap his face with a hairbrush. "This is such a gentle place," she said. "The meadowlarks sing. The doves do their mournful calls in the trees. A rooster or two brags, a hen cackles. Milk cows moo. All the different sounds I have heard are like music—soothing music."

"Wait till they play their instruments tonight. Then there will be real music."

"I hope so. But I've fallen in love with this place." She began to scrape his face.

Head back, he sat still. When she wiped the blade clean on a towel, he said, "It is an island in a sea of brown grass."

"Yes, it is." And went back to shaving him.

Two milk-fat goats were being cooked. Great pans of chopped onion, sweet peppers, and hot peppers were being roasted. Several women came and began to make tortillas of wheat flour and corn on griddles they brought and fired with mesquite sticks. Squatted around their work, they chattered in Spanish. Some young and pregnant, others with small babies, some older and bossier. For the most part they had grown up in this place or nearby or been brought as brides here.

Slocum enjoyed the red wine Juanita brought him and lay back in the shaded hammock catching some of the women's words. "—oh, she is pregnant at last—" "They worked hard at it." Laughter, and a sage voice. "Good thing it doesn't happen every time." More laughter.

He wondered about his friend and those invaders. Sounded to him like the gentle pastoral people here were being edged out of their grass by gunfighters and high-handed ranchers. It was a long ride to Santa Fe to complain. Most of the lawmen in this land were like the people, quiet spoken, not accustomed to handling hard cases who were gun-handy.

Their fathers and grandfathers had repelled the Comanche and Apache for centuries. It was a location too dry and unwanted by dirt farmers, most of whom passed by wondering how anyone lived out here and then hurried on their way to California. First the Spanish flag flew over them, then the Mexican one, and now the stars and stripes—and they remained tending their flocks and cattle, growing produce and hay in their plots, and living much as their ancestors had since the king sent them up the Rio Grande to homestead this hostile land.

Slocum could see the cross on top of the small chapel where the priest came by every third or fourth Sunday. Inside, candles were lit for special needs as these men and women sought help from the Virgin Mary and the saints and prayed on their own to cleanse their souls and prepare themselves for another week in the priest's absence. Their religion supported the community.

But they also partied hard at the drop of a hat. Fandangos, fiestas all brought music, special food, laughter, and excitement to these people living in the dust. Slocum looked forward to the evening, recalling many he'd attended as a buffalo hunter.

He remembered one such fandago when he'd met Antonieta. He'd forgotten her last name. They'd been eight weeks out hunting without a bath or a good meal. They'd brought several hundred hides back, stacked six feet high on the oxcarts. They were hoping to soon be rich and they reached the Rancho del Norte in a blizzard. Dry snow flew past like a swarm of moths at a light as they fell in the door of the small cantina, more like grizzly bears than snow-covered men with a thirst and a hard-on.

"Ah, Señors, welcome to Rancho del Norte."

Big Jim Donovan looked around and nodded. He was the only black man in the outfit. They waited for his real reply. "My, my, you's got a fire. Going to warm my hands." He pulled off the fringed gloves some squaw made for him, tucked them under his armpit, and held his fingers out to the fireplace's crackling oak blaze. "I'd done give a couple of hides fur this fire last night."

Everyone laughed and began to take off their stinking buffalo and bearskin coats. Slocum had not noticed the powerful aroma that they produced until the rise in temperature. The body odors coming off him made him wonder if he'd ever wiped his own ass in two months.

"Whiskey," O'Neal said, and made a sweeping gesture down the short bar.

The little man called Arturo set up the bottles and glasses on the bar. "Two bits a shot," he announced, and everyone nodded. He noted the contents of each bottle and charged them for the amount they drank. Not a bad price for rich men. Not too bad whiskey either.

The first drink cut the smoky taste from eating roasted buffalo hump twice a day out of Slocum's mouth. They only had two big meals while out hunting—morning and night. The first one was before dawn and the last after sundown in the short days of winter. Slocum looked around the narrow building and motioned Arturo over.

"Is there a barbershop here?"

"No, but the señora, she might help you."

"Where's this señora live?"

Arturo held his hand up like an ax and when it fell, it indicated south of the cantina. "Last casa."

"Last casa, huh?"

"Right, she is a very fine lady, the señora."

"She have a name?"

"Ah, yes, Antonieta."

With a confused nod, Slocum went and put on his coat. Campfire smoke and the constant cold and buffalo hunting had taken something out of him. His mind wasn't clear—he stumbled around a lot.

"Where you going?" O'Neal asked him when he was dressed.

"Going to see a woman about a bath and a shave. You got my bar bill?"

"Hell, yes," O'Neal said with the ends of his wet whiskers in his mouth. "Don't freeze your pecker off out there. I ain't taking a bath till springtime, if I do then."

Slocum nodded and went outside. He led his horse after himself. Damn, the heat inside had made him forget how bitterly cold it was outside. At the house, he hitched his pony at the yard gate and walked through the crunchy snow to the front door. Wind whistled around the fur cap on his head when he knocked wondering if anyone could hear it.

"Oh, come in," the short woman who opened the door said.

"Antonieta?" he asked.

"No, I will get the señora."

"Wait," he said, looking around at the tile floors and a fine painting of a matador on the wall. "There may be a mistake. Arturo said—"

"What did Arturo say?" The woman who came in was six feet tall with blond hair to her shoulders and large blue eyes. She walked toward him like a weeping willow tree in a gentle wind. The dark red dress was swirling around her legs. With no hesitation, she stuck her hand out.

He kissed it. "I am so sorry. I asked about a barbershop and he sent me here."

"You must have ridden an animal here?"

"Yeah, ole Pecos. It's out there." He indicated over his shoulder.

"Why don't you put him in my barn and hay and grain him. Ruby and I will begin to heat some water. No need to knock, come in the back door when you finish with him and we'll be getting ready for you."

How organized she was. "Yes, ma'am."

He put his fur cap back on, tied it down, and went outside. She smiled and closed the door after him. It must have been zero out there. He led Pecos around to the barn, shoved the door aside, put him in a tie stall, threw him some hay—that pony didn't know what grain was. He put the saddle and pads on a divider and took his .50-caliber Sharps in the buckskin sheath with him to the house.

Inside, he could see there was an entry room to leave his coat, cap, scarf, and leggings. He was busy putting it all up on wall pegs when she opened the door to the room a notch and smiled at him. "You must have found everything, Señor?"

"I sure hate stinking up your fine house," he said, coming inside and combing his stiff hair back with his fingers.

"*No problema.* We always enjoy company, Señor."

"Slocum, that's my name."

"Slo-cum," she pronounced it with a Spanish accent.

"Yes, ma'am." The kitchen smelled of cooking—things like onions and peppers and spices made his mouth water even standing there.

"When did you eat last?"

"Yesterday. We pushed hard to get here with the storm coming on."

"My goodness, why, you must be starved." She frowned at him.

"I'd rather get cleaned up first so I could savor it."

She nodded. "Come with me." She opened the door to an adjoining room. The copper tub steamed with hot water. A chair was set beside it, towels and a robe lay across it.

"I will rinse you when you get ready. Call me."

"I can—"

"I have seen men before. Have no fear and call me."

"Yes, ma'am." He toed off his boots to get undressed.

"My name is Antonieta. No ma'am, please?"

"Yes," he said as she exited the room with a high-handed wave. It made him shake his head in disbelief. He undressed, slipped into the tub, and held his breath—the water was hot. The heat from the small open fireplace reflected off him. He closed his eyes and savored the water's warmth seeking his tense muscles. Damn, this might be his best bath ever.

He got as low down as he could in the tub made for smaller men than him. Then he lathered and rubbed the bar of fine-smelling soap over every inch of his hide. When the water began to cool, he finally called to her. "Antonieta."

She slipped into the room with a pail of water. "I hope this is warm enough."

"It'll be fine," he said, and rose up out of the water, which brought on gooseflesh. Then she tipped the hot water over his head and it cascaded down him.

"Use the robe and bring the chair. I'll cut your hair and do it in the living room. It is the warmest room I have."

"My clothes?"

"Ruby will wash them."

"Yes, ma—I mean yes."

She smiled and went to the doorway before she turned back. "I will be waiting."

"Not long." He laughed and dried himself briskly. Then, in the robe, he padded out with the high-back chair for the living room. He found her ready with a pan of steaming water, a shaving cup, and bristle. She stropped a strap with a razor. "Ah, you are clean at last."

"Yes, for the first time in two months."

"You've been buffalo hunting?"

"No other reason for staying out there that long otherwise."

Busy lathering his face, she smiled at him. "I'll be anxious to see what you look like."

"Homely as anyone else."

"I doubt that." She finished the task of sharpening her blade and began to test it. Then, cleaning her blade of the white foam and hair on a towel over her arm, she set in to shave him.

"Married? Widow?" he asked.

"My husband left three years ago with a fourteen-year-old mistress. He was never heard of again. The courts have declared him dead. Of course, I have thought all along that the Comanche got him and her."

"So you remained?"

"I remained because this is all that was left of my husband's inheritance."

"The rest?"

"The rest he must have taken with him when he ran off." She smiled looking at his close-shaven face for anything she'd missed. "The girl"—she lowered her voice—"was Ruby's only daughter. She was pregnant at the time according to him. Something I couldn't give him—an heir."

When she handed Slocum the small mirror, he nodded in approval. "Get my mane trimmed, I may look human."

"That's next," she said, and threw the sheet over him.

In a short time she finished, and he looked at his image in the mirror and decided he did look human again.

"No wife? No family?" she asked.

"None. The war and what happened following it sent me off. Got in some scrapes. No place for me to plant my feet now."

She shook her head. The locks of blond hair waved like drapes around her face. "Such a shame. You look very nice cleaned up."

"My clothes will be dry—"

"You are in a hurry?"

"No—no, Antonieta. I am in no hurry to leave your company."

"Your clothes are a mess. Ruby is going to patch your britches with deerskin. The knees and seat are out. The elbows in the shirt are gone. You can wear a dead man's clothing for a while?"

"I'm not superstitious."

"Good, I'll get you some."

He watched her move away like a small dust devil, turning on her heels for the back of the house. Watching her move made his guts roil. What a lovely sight. Or was he so starved for a woman's body, he couldn't see her flaws? Damn, he felt clean outside, but his mind still wasn't thinking clearly. How could he ever open all his senses again?

Huddled against the cold, day in day out, night in night out, every waking hour watching over his shoulder for some slinking Kiowa or Comanch buck who wanted his hair, rifle, and horse—damn would he ever get back to normal?

"Here." She held out the pants and shirt. "They may be a little large, but they'll do."

He nodded and waited for her to turn away so he could dress.

"I want to see how bad they fit," she said, and handed him the shirt.

What the hell? He shed the robe and took the shirt. The heat from the fireplace sought his bare butt as she helped him into the shirt. It was big, but no problem. Obviously an expensive shirt. He took the pants next, and they proved much too big at the waist. She winked and began to put suspenders on them while he held them up by the waist. "This will keep them up."

"Yes."

"I have sent Ruby home. I hope you like lamb chops?"

"Sounds wonderful."

"You are too easy to please."

"No, I appreciate the clothing and all you have done for me." He followed her to the kitchen, where the table was set for them with wine poured in crystal glasses.

"To your good fortune with your sale of hides," she toasted him.

He nodded and they clinked glasses.

"You get many customers?" he asked passing her the plate of browned chops.

She laughed. "No. Arturo is very particular. Last one was a U.S. marshal looking for a murderer. That was last spring."

He shook his head, "I merely wondered."

"Of course, the crazy black widow who kills her prey, huh?"

"I've never a seen blond Spanish woman before."

"Come to northern Spain. I have many counterparts."

He nodded. The food melted in his mouth, the red wine washed it down, and he ate more—not believing he was really in her house looking into her blue eyes, which looked deeper than any ocean.

Then, as if someone unseen had begun to play a violin, they both rose and he took her in his arms and they swung around the kitchen to the inaudible music. Who needed the music? It was inside each of them. Finally, he released her hand—he leaned forward and kissed her pouty lower lip. Their arms flew around each other as they sought each other in a hard hug. His need for her was so blinding he couldn't hold back.

She pushed the suspenders off his shoulders and the pants fell to his knees.

"Here?" he asked, holding her hips hard against his.

"No, in my bed," she said, looking sleepy-eyed at him and pushing back his short bangs.

Long pear-shaped breasts capped with brown pointed nipples sent him into a frenzy he tried to control. But their eagerness was shared, and they rolled locked in each other's arms under the down covers in the high bed. Then she parted her long shapely legs under him and he raised up. He slid home, and she cried out when he stretched her ring.

"Oh, take me, take me," she cried with her head thrown back and her throat exposed.

He did, and they became a wild machine. His knees were on fire from the friction as he fought to go deeper and deeper. His erection sensed every nerve ending. They went forever and ever, until at last he felt the needles in his butt and grasped her in preparation.

"Yes, yes," she huffed, and looked down between them as if watching for him to finish. Her chin flew up when the fire started, and she dug her fingernails into him. Her legs straightened and she cried out when he came. They lay in each other's arms exhausted and content.

They woke each other up and made love off and on all night.

Dawn came through the frosted windowpanes in a prism of gold, orange, and red and the wind was down. A rooster crowed, and Slocum sat up rubbing his face with his calloused palms. He could smell her musk on him. The soft perfume tickled his nose, but he at last could see clearly—his mind was working. He snuggled against her warm body, reached over, fondled her breast, and smiled to himself—he was well again.

6

"Wake up," Belle said, and shook him with a grin. "Don Jeminez just rode in."

"Oh," he said, and threw his legs over the side of the bed. It was late afternoon and the shadows from the house extended way past him. He stood up and stretched, stealing a kiss from her. It caused her to blush.

"There is a room in the barn. Juanita and I cleaned it this afternoon for us."

"Good. I better go see my friend."

She agreed.

He strapped on his six-gun and adjusted it. Halfway around the house he heard the ring of someone running with spurs.

"*Mi amigo.*" They hugged and beat each other on the back in a cloud of dust.

"When did you get here?" Don Jeminez asked.

"Earlier."

"Where are you going?"

"To Texas, to find a man who killed Belle's husband."

"You look good. I wonder often where you are and how you are doing."

Slocum swept off his friend's hat to look at his head.

58

"A little snow on the mountain but there must be fire inside."

"A big fire," Jeminez said, and put his arm on Slocum's shoulder.

"These Texans are pushing you."

"That is a nice word. Our land has no fences, so we can't keep them out, but they will eat all the grass and then sell their cattle and we will have no grass left for ours."

"What has the law done?"

"They sent a deputy up here, but he can't do anything but complain to them when we show him that their cattle are on our land. He says we must fence it, and then when they cut it he can arrest them."

"How would he catch them?" Slocum asked amused.

"He couldn't. Every day I drive their steers back east, but there are many I can't find and send back."

"I'll see if Belle can wait a few days and maybe I can help you."

"They have many gunhands. I think they will use them when they want more range."

Slocum nodded and they took seats on the porch bench. "Maybe we can discourage them."

"These men are killers. You kill them, more will come." His knees spread apart, Jeminez leaned forward and began to whittle on a piece of red cedar with a long-bladed jackknife. "You said a woman is with you."

"Her name is Belle Nelson. She's from Wyoming. Bounty hunters shot her husband thinking he was a wanted man. She wants the last one's hide nailed to the outhouse wall."

"He is in Texas?" Jeminez sat up and straightened. Slocum noticed he was thinner than in his buff-hunting days. He had more lines around his eyes and the look of an old wolf—wiser too.

"I'm not saying call them out for a shoot-out. I'm saying tie a tin can on their tail and send them home."

Jeminez blinked his brown eyes at him. "How would you do that?"

"Oh, load some of their firewood with explosives. Cut some cinches in two. Replace some good whiskey with bad. You make a man wonder if ghosts are after him, he can come to believe it after a while; even tough gunslingers take notice. They can't shoot the air full of holes."

With a soft chuckle, Jeminez nodded. "When do we start?"

Slocum looked across the rolling country beyond the wall. "A scarecrow. You know where we can find a skull?"

His brows furrowed, Jeminez shook his head as if that would never work. "No."

Slocum rose, stretched. "I'll ask Juanita."

"How would she know of such a thing?" Jeminez folded up his jackknife and slid it in his pocket, getting up to follow Slocum inside.

"A skull?" Juanita said when they found the women in the kitchen.

"We need a skull for a scarecrow."

"How about a small melon carved like one?" She looked to Belle, who nodded.

"Good," he said. "A sombrero and an old sheet. I'll make the note to pin on it. You have an old holster and belt?"

"What will you do with it?"

"Scare some Texans," he said with his arm over Belle's shoulder.

Belle smiled and then frowned. "You're going to scare that bunch of Texans with a scarecrow?"

"That and other things. Make a man nervous enough and he might shoot himself in the foot." Slocum grinned at her.

While the women worked on the head and sheet, Slocum and Don Jeminez went to the barn to select three sticks from Jeminez's stock of fence stays to make a tripod, and a short stick for the dummy's shoulders. In a few hours, the scarecrow was assembled in the backyard with a melon face painted white, the cuts for eyes, nose, and mouth full of charcoal. They made a sign that read MUERTE, MUERTE, TE-JANOS, to pin on him after they set him up.

"Where will we put him?" Don asked.

"Just outside of their base camp where they can't miss him."

"How will that scare them?" Juanita asked with her hands on her hips.

"All we need to do is start to unnerve them," Slocum said. "Then they'll scare themselves."

"I hope it works."

"It will. Let's look at your wood supply."

"Sure, amigo, what do you need?" Don Jeminez asked with a frown.

"Some pieces that have a hollow center." Slocum went with him to the woodpile.

"Ah, you are going to make a bomb. I have a small keg of gunpowder I refill my pistol with."

"Good. We plug the ends of the hollow sticks and make them look natural, then fill them with gunpowder and that will wake the Texans up."

Slocum selected the wood sticks, finding several.

A newspaper plug was inserted several inches inside each hole so it was not obvious, then the granular black powder poured in and the other end plugged discreetly too. With a bundle of the sticks bound up, Slocum nodded and clapped his friend on the shoulder. "Where can I find a case of blasting-powder sticks?"

"Maybe at the mine?"

"And that's?"

"Oh, on Blue Mesa. I know the owner, Frank Keating. He'll sell us some. I bought some before to blow up a beaver dam. What will we do with that?"

"Save it for later."

Jeminez nodded slowly and scratched his ear. "And if this does not move them—"

"Then we get tougher."

"I must tell my neighbors tonight what we plan. They will worry, but they know if we don't stop the Texans soon, we won't have any grass for our cattle and sheep."

"Then we need to make some wide sweeps and head their cattle back east," Slocum said.

After the festive fandango, when they were in their bed in the tack room, Belle asked, "How can I help you?"

"I guess you can ride along if you want to."

"Good. I want to go too." She snuggled closer. "Now we have a bed—" Her hand rubbed his belly and drifted lower. Soon she was waking his dick.

He rolled over and scooted closer. "Yes, now we need to play." He kissed her until anxiety had him wild with desire and they made love.

At dawn they started for the mine, Don Jeminez talking sharply to his stiff-legged red saddle mule named Tonto, which meant "stupid." Jeminez was doing lots of scolding to keep it from bucking as it danced on eggs out the gate and across the grassland headed north.

Belle was amused and chuckled. "Bet he can buck too."

"He ever thrown you?" Slocum asked aloud.

"*Sí*, plenty." But Jeminez managed to settle him down and they rode for the distant mesa.

"This a gold mine we're going to?" she asked as the three rode abreast.

"No, it's a coal mine."

Jeminez's mule was in a stiff trot, flicking his long reddish ears all around as if listening for bogeymen. Slocum's bay was in a long trot he could hold all day, and Belle's good gray was in an easy slow lope. They managed to move at the same ground-eating speed, and the coolness of the day swept Slocum's face as they flushed meadowlarks and bobwhites and darting long-tail chaparrals.

As they came over a rise, several longhorn steers raised their heads.

"Their cattle," Don Jeminez said, and made an angry hard face at the lot as the riders moved away in a trot.

Slocum nodded, looking the longhorn crosses over. "They need those four-year-olds fat to ship them this fall."

"On our grass too."

"When will you tell the others?"

"Tonight, I called for a meeting."

"Good. Let's lope." They set out, and by mid-morning reached the mine.

Keating was a big man with coal dust in his skin. He came outside the clapboard office, took off a felt hat, and wiped his face on a blue shirtsleeve. "Hey, Jeminez, what brings you up here?"

Slocum didn't miss his careful look at Belle. Most men didn't miss her good looks and shapely figure, even when she was in men's clothing.

"Ah," Jeminez said, "I need to do some blasting, Frank."

"Got them damn beavers again?" Then Frank shook his head and looked hard at her. "Sorry, ma'am. I don't get many lady folks up here."

"No problem."

"I got beavers," Jeminez said, and dismounted.

"I'm Tom White and this is Belle," Slocum said as he and Belle both dismounted, anxious to stand on the ground after the hard ride.

"Well, Tom, any friend of Jeminez is a friend of mine." They shook hands and everyone went in to the office.

Slocum had noted the piles of coal outside. The man had a large supply on hand. "Coal business good these days?"

Keating shook his head. "I need rail lines to ship it. Only way I can get a spur up here is give them twenty-five percent of my mine."

"Don't they need coal?" Slocum asked.

"Say they can get it up in Colorado. All they want. And I can't freight enough coal out by wagons to make a living."

"What does that mean?"

"Guess I'll give them a quarter of it. They asked for sixty percent the first time."

"A spur would mean we could ship cattle from here," Jeminez said, looking pleased.

"If they don't ask for a quarter of them," Keating said.

After lunch they left for the rancheria, with the blasting sticks in sacks tied behind Slocum's cantle.

They arrived at Jeminez's place by supper time, and ate hurriedly to get ready for the meeting in the town square. Jeminez acted concerned, and Slocum finally asked if it would be better if he didn't go to the meeting since he was an outsider.

"No, I will need all the help I can get."

Slocum kissed Belle on the forehead and followed Jeminez out when it was time to go. The sun was down and twilight had set in across New Mexico. They went to the square. Several men had already taken seats on the benches or squatted in a semicircle.

Raul Mendoza, the leader, spoke first. "We have a big problem. These cattle are eating all our feed. Twice"—he held up two fingers—"I have ridden to talk to the Texans, but they only scoff at our claims and say there is no fence.

"I know we are not *pistoleros,* but the sheriff says he does not have enough men to stop them." Mendoza shook his head and looked down at the ground.

"What can we do?" another man asked. "We are herders and farmers. These *tejanos* have many gunhands and will kill us." He shook his head in defeat. "I have a family. If I am dead, who will care for my wife and little ones?"

"You say give them the grass and let our own stock starve this winter?" Jeminez asked, then sat down in disgust.

"We can sell them this fall and buy back more when the *tejanos* are gone."

"Yes, we can do that," several others agreed.

Slocum rose and waited until Mendoza asked him to speak. "I know these Texans. You do that and they will stay forever on your land."

"We can get the judge to tell them to leave. He told us this was our land."

Slocum shook his head. "No, then they will fight you in court for years, and that will cost thousands in fees and you could even lose."

"Señor, what should we do?" one older man asked.

"Tie a tin can on their tails and send them home."

"No. No. They will kill us!" someone shouted. Many joined in.

"I won't die like a dog in my bed," Jeminez said. "I won't cower from these mangy curs. Do as you wish."

"You will bring their wrath down upon us," one man shouted.

The meeting broke up with Mendoza pleading for more time. Slocum and his friend walked back.

"What do you wish to do?" Slocum asked softly, realizing Jeminez's disappointment over the failure of the community to rise up and help run the Texans off.

"Go ahead with our plans."

"You're certain?"

"Yes. We can ride tonight and begin."

"Then we will." Slocum clapped him on the shoulder. "It would have been easier to have had the help."

"I have failed you. I thought I could get them to help us."

"No problem, my friend. We can whip these Texans," Slocum said. "You seen a dead snake around here?"

"Why?"

"I want it to spice their water barrel."

"There's a big rattler hung on the fence by the bean patch. I saw it yesterday."

"Good, we'll get it riding out."

They loaded the scarecrow on pack mules and saddled

their own animals. Belle wanted to go too, not convinced
that she should do as he'd suggested—stay behind. Finally
she agreed to stay, and the two men rode out. Slocum gathered the rattler, which already smelled bad. With the snake
in a sack, he booted his nervous horse on. It would be a
long night.

They found the cowboys' camp and crept close. Slocum
found no guard when he crept on his belly near the scattered bedrolls and the wagon. He went back for Jeminez,
and they quietly put the explosive wood on top of the cowboys' woodpile, then drew back to the wagon. Slocum
lifted the wooden lid on the water barrel as quietly as he
could and slipped the stinking serpent into the liquid. Then
the two men eased away from the snoring cowboys for
their own horses and the mule hitched in a wash.

Slocum had figured that the cowboys would have a
nighthawk with the horses, but there was no sign of him. In
a grove of mesquite, they set up the scarecrow about thirty
feet from the wagon tracks and less than a quarter mile
from camp. When the night wind ruffled him, the dummy
looked a little spooky in the starlight.

Their work completed, they chose a ridge east of the
camp to observe what happened. They were high enough to
see things at a distance with Slocum's glasses. The horses
and mule were hobbled behind them in a draw. Then the
two men bellied down and waited. Slocum slept a few
winks until Jeminez woke him.

"Horses are coming in."

Slocum rolled over and took a look. To the ringing of
the bell mare, the pounding of hooves, and the sound of
horses snorting in the dust, the wrangler brought the herd
in. Then someone lit a lantern at the tailgate of the wagon
where a canvas cover shaded things. Even their voices carried in the night.

"—start a fire."

Slocum smiled. *Yeah, a big one.*

Kettles clanged. From the tinny sound, it was obvious that the coffeepot was being filled, and there was the clang of a Dutch oven lid as it was moved to the work area.

"Fire's going. . . ."

"Better get them up."

"Yeah." The ring of the triangle carried across the land. Dark forms in the faint predawn light staggered to the perimeter of the camp and pissed long streams off into the shadowy bunchgrass. As they shook their peckers off and put them away, their sleep-graveled voices began to carry.

Two squatting cowboys mooned the prairie dogs and grunted in their bowel movements. But they jerked up when the first charged stick went off in the campfire. The clap came with a sharp flare, and then things became quiet.

"What the fuck was that?"

"Who's been screwing with my wood?" an angry voice demanded.

"None of us."

"Well, if I have any more—"

The wood began to explode. A large red flare went up in the air higher than the wagon top and exploded. Others sticks began spewing fire at the men close by. They all ran and hit the ground. They must have lit every loaded stick in the camp. The explosions stampeded their horses, and even the nighthawk's pony left too.

The nighthawk ran after them screaming, "Come back, damn you!"

The air was blue with cursing. Both Jeminez and Slocum ducked back under the hill suppressing their own laughter to snickers.

"Let's go," Slocum said. "Their horses ran north. We can skirt south and they'll miss us."

"What about the scarecrow?"

"They may find him while chasing down their horses."

Slocum chuckled. The outfit was going to find out things weren't all roses in New Mexico. There would be some thorns.

They short-loped back to the ranch as the first rays of sun came up over the horizon. Shots in the distance made Slocum smile and turn to Jeminez. "They've shot the scarecrow."

They both laughed and pushed their mounts on.

In the late afternoon they rode through the gate. Belle came running with a six-gun in her hand. No one was in the square. Slocum searched around with his hand on his gun butt, then dismounted.

She swept the hair from her face. "The enforcers were here at sunup. The leader and several of his hard cases."

"What did they do?"

"Made everyone come down here and told them if anyone drove any MC steer even one foot, they'd shoot them and then come back here and rape every woman and child in this village."

A wave of rage swept over Slocum. "What's the leader's name?"

"Jerry Booth."

The name meant nothing to him. "What happened?"

"Everyone went and hid in their houses when the enforcers rode out."

"Like cowards," Jeminez said in disgust.

"No, they are just afraid, and I would be too."

"But—"

"I know," Slocum said. "They are farmers and herders, not gunfighters. We need to shut Booth and his rannies off."

Jeminez agreed and they headed for his house leading their horses. Slocum looked back over the deserted square—it would be a long fight.

7

Slocum lay on his belly in the grass under the tan blanket. He could hear the two cowboys talking as they rode up to the water hole.

"You seen anything?"

"Nothing, but a damned ole slinking coyote since we left camp this morning."

"Boss said be on the lookout."

"For what—"

"Get your hands high," Slocum ordered emerging from under his cover with a gun in his fist. Jeminez came from the other side and covered the shocked-looking pair as Slocum disarmed them.

One was an older man with gray hair, the other a kid.

"Now get your money out and put it on the ground."

"You—you robbing us?" the kid asked looking like a cornered animal.

"No, but you'll need it where you're going."

The older man frowned. "Where we going?"

"Get your clothes off and we'll tell you."

"Huh?"

Slocum pointed the Colt at him. "I said get undressed and now."

69

"My Gawd, this is stupid—"

"Just undress or I'll bust you over the head and jerk them off."

The two disgruntled cowboys undressed down to their underwear. Jeminez bundled up their clothing and boots.

"Now pick up your money," Slocum ordered.

"I never—"

"Shut up. You two start walking to Campo and get a ride out of this country if you know what's good for you."

"In our socks?"

"Don't make him mad, Tom," the kid said, tugging on his sleeve.

"Right, and if we catch you punching for the MC again, I don't have to tell you what we'll do to you."

"What the hell you want our damn clothes for?"

Slocum shook his head and motioned them on with his gun barrel. "Head for Campo."

"Come on, Tom, least he didn't shoot us," the kid said.

Gingerly they made high steps headed northwest. With the cowboys' clothes bundled and tied on their horses, Slocum and Jeminez headed for their camp. The women were busy stuffing some clothing with dry grass when they reached the canvas shade strung between some cottonwoods. In fact, the first dummy looked real enough as it leaned against a tree trunk.

"You tied a can on two more?" Belle asked looking up.

"That's four less punchers they've got."

"That last one, might go back to the cow camp," Jeminez said, tossing down the men's clothing.

Slocum agreed and joined in with Belle stuffing the hay inside the next set of clothes. "He acted about half cranky over this deal."

"Again, how do you plan to use these scarecrows?" Belle asked.

"We'll strap them on their horses and stampede them right into their camp."

"Will that scare them?" Bell asked with a flannel shirt half full in her lap.

"Combined with blasting sticks and not knowing where the missing hands are, it will all help."

"When do we do it?"

"In the morning."

"Well, then, you two better get to stuffing or it won't be done," Juanita said.

By sundown, the four stuffed dummies were completed, with sack and hats stitched on their white cloth faces. Slocum and the others sat on the ground cross-legged and ate frijoles and beef wrapped in Juanita's flour tortillas.

"Why do this in such a hurry?" Juanita asked, ready to take a bite of her burrito.

"If they don't know where those four cowboys are at, then they'll be upset about them not coming in. Then a raid on their camp at daybreak will make some of them upset enough to clear out."

Juanita nodded. "I better go home in the morning and check on things, unless you three need me."

"We'll be all right. But be careful that Booth hasn't got some men posted there."

"I can go in the back way."

"She knows how to sneak in," Jeminez said, and gave her a friendly push. Everyone laughed.

They set everything up in the dark of night. Slocum arranged the blasting sticks in a row on the north side of the camp. Jeminez and Belle were in the south ready to stampede the horses and their dummies into camp.

The cook rang the triangle in the predawn darkness and Slocum prepared the first charge, then lit the long fuses for the others. He was on his horse, riding hard to the west when the first blast occurred. The exposion drew shouts and swear words as he set the horse down and waited for the next ones. It had spooked their remuda and men were trying to head the horses off when the series of blasts went off. Then, thundering out of the south, came four horses and riders—they were met with many gunshots and shouts of "Raid! Raid!"

Slocum loped his pony westward. Booth would have to think about this for a while. With four punchers gone, he'd have to convince the rest to stay. It would be a disease that worked on the mind until some of his gunmen would ease away in the night. It would work in time.

"They sure wasted lots of lead on those dummies," Belle said when she and Jeminez joined him.

"Adds to the idea that they have an unseen enemy," Slocum said as the sun began to emerge.

"What next?" Jeminez asked.

"They get supplies out of Texas?" Slocum asked.

"Yes, they send two freight wagons in from there every three weeks or so. I found that out from Pedro. He saw them the last two times when he rode over to Texas to see his uncle who works on a ranch across the line."

"When would the next trip be due?"

"I guess any day. Why?"

"If they don't have supplies, they might get hungry."

Jeminez nodded and smiled. "We stop the wagons."

Slocum nodded. "Belle and I'll scout for them tomorrow."

"They could get supplies in Campo," she said.

"Yes, but that would cost more. I'm sure the MC head man sends the supplies so he can save money."

"So what do we do to the supplies?" she asked.

"Make sure they don't get to Booth."

"You think I can take some boys and start pushing some of their cattle back?" Jeminez asked.

"Better wait till we get back. If we can cut down on Booth's numbers, we can start doing that."

Jeminez nodded. "I'll wait then."

The supply train, if they could find it in time, might be the best way to cut Booth off at the knees.

They rode into the rancho after sundown. Raul Mendoza hurried out to intercept them.

"Two Texas cowboys in their underwear came in to Campo today and said they had been robbed. Orando said they were the second pair who came in to town wearing only underwear."

"So?" Jeminez asked. "Who did such a thing?"

"They said *bandidos*." Raul spread out his hands.

"Where did they go?" Slocum asked.

"Back to Texas after they bought some clothes."

"They must have had money in their boots," Jeminez said.

"No, the *bandidos* stole them too. I think they went to the railroad. Someone took them in a buggy. The bartender said they told him they had enough of New Mexico."

Jeminez nodded his head in approval. "I would have too."

Slocum, Jeminez, and Belle rode on not daring to snicker until they were out of sight and hearing of the man.

At the barn, Slocum dropped heavily off his horse. "Four gone."

"How many more do you suspect will leave after this morning's raid?" Belle asked, and put her stirrup up on the seat to undo her girth.

"We've cut into his force. But hired guns are cheap. MC could send reinforcements if Booth sends word."

"Oh, you are back," Juanita said, and joined them at the corral. "There is a fiesta tonight."

Slocum nodded. "Sounds wonderful." They needed a break. He glanced back feeling that in this chess game between him and Booth, it was Booth's turn to move. When and how he would was the question.

The Chinese lanterns were lit and strung across the square. Men and women in their finest clothes came to the tables heaped with food to fill their plates. An oaken barrel of fine red wine was set up with a spigot and goblets were filled from it. Musicians tuned their fiddles and guitars and one man played the trumpet. The fiesta was for a young girl to celebrate her Confirmation.

Slocum squatted in the shadows on his boot heels and watched the fiesta begin under the flickering lights. Belle soon returned from the crowd with a plate of food for him.

"I hope you like it," she said.

"Anything you picked out I will love," he said and thanked her.

"They can sure party," she said as couples shuffled to the music on the hard-packed ground.

"That's how they've survived for centuries in such remote places."

The music filled the night. Small children, dressed in their Sunday best and sitting on blankets spread on the ground, were busy eating tortilla-wrapped food and chattering. In their naive ways they acted isolated from worldly things—an innocence that buffered them from the worries of adults.

"More cattle are drifting or being driven west. I heard them talking about it," Belle said seated beside him.

"Maybe they will finally realize what they are hiding from," he said, chewing on the mesquite-browned meat, peppers, and brown beans in a flour tortilla.

"They sounded upset."

He could only hope that they would be able to discourage the MC from continuing their push onto the ranch's land. If any of his plans worked, perhaps they could.

"I love this music and all but—" She looked over at him.

"But you would rather escape to somewhere else like our room?" He smiled at her.

"Yes." She chewed on her lower lip.

"I can eat on the way," he said in a soft voice.

"Wonderful."

8

On his belly, Slocum used his field glasses on the two wagons. The large MC painted on the side of the green wagon boxes told him enough. Both wagons were powered by double teams of large Missouri mules, the tobacco-spitting teamsters sharing their spring seats with young swampers. The barrel of a rifle stuck out of each wagon box close to the brake lever. Like the other hard cases that worked for the big outfit, these men were not the type to lie down and play dead.

"They don't have any guards." Jeminez looked hard across the grassland at the distant canvas tops.

"No, but those freighters aren't any pushovers."

"What should we do?"

"They're across the line in New Mexico, so we don't have to worry about the Texas authorities."

Jeminez nodded. "New Mexico can't even keep them off our land."

"My own idea of law here. I say we wake them tonight and send them packing."

"Sí, mi amigo."

They dropped back to their horses, hidden in the draw, and rode away. Belle was cooking some beans in camp when they rode up.

"Find them?"

"Yes, they'll camp at some springs tonight, Jeminez says."

"How many men?"

"Four, but two are swampers. They're not much to concern us. The drivers are knowledgeable, I figure."

The moon had been up for several hours when they located the four bedrolls around the campfire's coals. Squatted by the wagons, Slocum sent Belle to hold her gun on a swamper sleeping nearby. Jeminez was to take the driver on the left, Slocum the one snoring on the right.

Slocum soon squatted beside the noisy one and stuck his pistol muzzle in his face. "Get up slowlike or die."

With a strangled snore and a "Huh?" he bolted up wide-eyed at the bore of the Colt in his vision.

"Who in the fuck're you?"

"That's not important. Pull your boots on and get up."

"I ain't—"

"You want to walk back to the ranch barefoot, fine."

He scrambled to pull them on.

The two teamsters and their helpers were soon bound with their hands behind their backs and seated on the ground and under Belle's guard. Slocum found some jerky and brought it out to set beside them; then he filled a couple of canteens with water. Jeminez went and cut the hobbled mules loose.

Finding a few cans of coal oil, Slocum spread the flammable liquid over the contents of both wagons, then loaded the harness in the wagons.

"You, pick up those canteens and jerky and all four of you start walking for Texas. When these wagons blow up, you won't want to be near them."

"I don't know who you are, mister, but when the old man learns you done this, your life ain't worth a plugged nickel," a teamster said.

"Maybe his ain't either. Get walking. Get the horses," he said to Belle.

Jeminez had put the rifles and the ammo he found in the wagons in two sacks. He nodded in approval as the four marched off in the starlight. "No supplies this month."

They tied a sack on each saddle when Belle brought the horses up. Jeminez and Slocum carried an extra rifle.

"Ready to ride?" Slocum asked.

Jeminez and Belle nodded.

"Drive the mules ahead of you." Slocum drew two half sticks of fused blasting powder from his saddlebags and lit them. He waved Belle and Jeminez away, tossed one stick in each wagon, then galloped out to where they'd turned back to watch.

His first explosion sent flames up, lighting the canvas cover orange, then beginning to consume it. The second one blew up in a red ball of fire that rained down pieces in the glowing light. He nodded to the others and they rode off in the dark—misssion accomplished.

Two days later they were back at the ranchero. Juanita met them, coming out of the doorway with a strained look on her face. "They pistol-whipped the Ortega boy and stampeded his sheep."

"When?" Jeminez asked stepping off his mule.

"Yesterday. He rode in this morning. They really beat him up."

"What about the sheep?" Jeminez shared a disapproving look with Slocum.

"Raul and some of the others went right out to see about them."

"Good. Is the boy at his home?" Slocum asked.

"He is at his parents' jacal. He's not married."

Slocum dismounted and handed the reins to Belle. "We better go see how he is doing and who did this to him."

"We can put the horses up," Juanita said, and took the two extra rifles from them. "What about the supply wagons?"

"Poof," Jeminez said, and made an explosion with his fingers.

"Good," she said, and the men started out.

The boy's mother, Etta Ortega, a small gray-haired woman, showed them inside her casa. The young man, in his late teens, with his head bound up in bandages, was on a pallet, and a girl in her early teens was on her knees letting him sip something from a glass.

"This is his girlfriend, Julia," Jeminez said.

Squatting on his heels, Slocum looked hard at the youth. "Who were the men who beat you up?"

The boy shook his head. "They were cowboys. I did not know them."

"Ramon was not here when Booth came by and threatened them. He was out with his sheep," Jeminez said. "He's never seen him."

Slocum nodded. "Did the leader have a fancy red kerchief?"

"*Sí, señor.*"

"What did he say?"

"They were there to teach me a lesson. Don't graze my sheep where his cattle must graze." The boy closed his black eye and shook his head. "Where am I to go?"

"How many were there?"

"Three."

"Does that mean he lost some?" Jeminez asked.

"Too early to know for sure," Slocum said, in deep thought about how to handle this.

"What about the sheep?"

"They shot several and stampeded them away," said the boy, Ramon. "I must have passed out. My sheep were gone when I caught my burro to come back here. They were a good flock. I have worked many years on making them better. I fear they are all dead."

"He has many stitches," his mother said.

"I can see they really worked on him. Ramon, get well and we will even the score."

He forced a smile and nodded. "*Gracias*, and pray for my sheep."

"I will." Slocum rose and nodded to the young girl. "Get him well."

"*Sí*," she said, and applied a wet cloth to wipe his face.

"Who will they hurt next?" his mother asked.

"I don't know, but they will certainly keep trying until they move all of you off this ranchero."

"Never," she said, so cold it drove the day's heat out of the jacal.

"We will do what we can not to let that happen."

"God be with you," she said as they left her.

On the way back to Jeminez's place, they reflected on the raid.

"It is not the last one," Slocum said. "He expects these people to bend to his demands, and if they don't, he will enforce them."

"I agree, but what can I do with a camp full of cowards?"

"Just do what we can." Slocum shook his head. "We need to spook away some more of his hands."

"I bet the women have some food ready," Jeminez said as they went to wash up on the porch.

"How is the boy?" Belle asked from the doorway.

"They pistol-whipped him and he has several stitches and a bad black eye. He says that Booth was the leader and they ran off his sheep."

"What can we do for him?"

Slocum put his arm on her shoulder. "His girlfriend is there and she has things under control."

"All right. I think Juanita has some food ready."

"Good, we can always eat." Jeminez laughed and they went in to his house.

Late in the afternoon, Raul came by and gave them a report on the sheep herd. Ten were dead, a few more lost, but they had the rest and they were fine. The other two men were driving them back toward the ranch.

"How can we stop these Texans?" Raul asked, looking tired as he sat on the porch bench, elbows on his knees.

"Either pick at them like we have, or confront them."

"We are not soldiers—"

"Maybe you will have to be to ever save this place."

Raul nodded at Slocum's words and looked over at him. "But what have you two done?"

"Ran off some of their hands, upset their camp, and stopped their supply wagons from reaching them."

Blinking his eyes, Raul shook his head. "But they still struck and hurt that boy."

"They want your range and won't quit till they get it. Piece by piece, they will force you off this land."

"I believe Slocum," Jeminez said. "This is not just to graze on our land this year, but from now on."

"The judge said our claim was valid."

Slocum looked around. "I don't see him or any deputies around here to help you. Didn't the last one say you must fence it?"

"Yes. No way we could afford to do that." Raul looked defeated.

"This one who owns the MC knows that too."

"Who is he?"

"Some high roller trying to build an empire," said Slocum.

"I don't savvy that."

"He means he wants to be king over our land," Jeminez said, and Slocum agreed.

"Long ago," Raul began, "my great-grandfather came here with ten *carretas,* five other families, and a dozen soldiers armed with lancers. They brought sheep, cattle, horses, and took hold of this land grant. They fought the Comanche and Apache to hold this—what must we do now?"

"Since the law won't help, then the people must become the law," Slocum said.

"But how?"

"Take the fight to them."

"We are not pistoleros. Few of us have guns."

"Then we need to change that and arm everyone. We have some extra weapons we've taken from the Texans and some ammo. We need a half-dozen more rifles and ammunition for them."

"What if we fail and all get killed?"

Slocum looked him in the eye. "It won't matter then."

Raul collapsed on the bench. "I will call a meeting and we will tell them this time the truth."

"You will be lucky if they don't tell you no," Jeminez said to Raul, then rose and stalked away.

Slocum stood up and stretched. "Good luck."

"I will need it," said Raul.

Slocum found his friend working on replacing a latigo on his saddle in the shade of a rustling cottonwood. He was obviously angry and upset as he jerked and slapped the leather around.

"Raul may convince them," Slocum said.

"No, they are all cowardly coyotes." Jeminez shook his head vehemently "They will say, oh, he will come and beat me like he did the boy." With his fist, he jerked the new latigo hard to test his tie. Satisfied, he tossed the strap on the resting saddle. "I live with cowards in this place. I may move away. I am ashamed to say they are even my people. Maybe I am not even one of them."

"I recall that winter we froze our asses off buffalo hunting and you complained that none of your own brothers would come out there and risk hunting."

"And, *mi amigo,* I made the money to start ranching that winter. They still work like peons in Santa Fe at making and laying adobe bricks for another man. I have little use for them either."

Slocum chewed on a hay stem. "These people here may surprise you."

Jeminez shook his head. "In the morning, I am taking my .50-caliber Sharps and declaring open season on them. Anyone herding cattle on the grant land can expect to die."

"Maybe we ought to offer Booth that information."

"What, and have him swoop down and burn this village?" Jeminez asked. "I am going to show him."

"I think the people here would be interested in at least defending it."

"We will see tonight."

Raul came on the run and both men looked up. "I have the money for six more rifles. Would you two go into Campo and buy them?"

"Sure," Slocum said. "Get the extra two that Juanita has in the house and a box of ammo for each of them. Post as guards some men that can shoot."

Raul handed Slocum the buckskin purse. "Yes. I will feel better when you return."

"It will be after dark. Jeminez, go tell the women and we'll ride." Slocum hoisted his saddle off the rack and went for his horse.

In minutes they were saddled under the anxious eyes of the two women. He hugged and kissed Belle, told her to stay close to her guns. She gave him a grave nod to indicate she would, and they rode out.

The sun was red in the sky in the west when they reached Campo and dismounted at the mercantile. Their horses hitched at the rack, Slocum looked over the shadows in the ruby glare. Nothing looked out of place. They entered the store as a young man lit the lamps and raised them up.

"You have six .44/40 Winchesters?" Slocum asked.

"They're sold," the young man said, blowing out the match and climbing off the chair.

"You mean you have six rifles in the case and they're sold?"

"Yes, sir, the MC Cattle Company bought them over a week ago."

"He pay you cash?"

"No, sir. Mr. Booth put them on their account."

"Good, you can order him some more. I have the cash." Slocum pounded the money bag on the counter.

"I can order you more, but they'll be three or four weeks getting here."

"Good, then Booth can take those."

"But these are sold—"

"Son, I don't give a damn." Slocum leaned across the counter to get closer to him. "Count my money."

"But Mr. Booth said—"

"What did he say?"

"Ah, ah, don't sell any rifles to any Mexicans."

"I guess he is going to buy all the others."

The boy swallowed hard. "He did. All the pistols and ammo too."

Slocum held his arm out to keep Jeminez from exploding. "Do I look Mexican?"

"No—no—sir."

"Count the money." Slocum took the purse by the bottom and spilled the coins on the counter.

The boy herded them in a pile with his shaking hands. And he began to count out loud. "Ten, twenty, thirty-five—"

"Get the case of rifles," he said to Jeminez.

Trembling and close to crying, the boy shook his head. "I can't let you have them."

"Too bad. How much you have there?"

Jeminez dragged the box out and lifted the lid to count them. "They're all here."

"Money there?" Slocum demanded of the boy.

"Booth may kill me." The boy snuffed his nose and his lashes were wet with tears.

"Not if we have our way. Is there enough money on this counter for the rifles and some ammo?"

"Yes—six boxes—" He swallowed hard and bit his lower lip.

Slocum slapped down more money. "Make it six more."

The boy stacked them on the counter from underneath. "Why—what will I tell Booth?"

"His shipment will be here in a month."

"But—but—"

Slocum grasped him by the shirt and pulled him close. "Ask him what cemetery he wants them delivered at."

"Oooh—"

"I'll go get a packhorse from Abe," Jeminez said, looking over at the ammunition and the wooden box of rifles on the floor. "We'll need one."

"Reckon he'll sell one to a Mexican?" Slocum laughed after him as he ran out the door.

"He damn sure better," Jeminez said over his shoulder.

The boy collapsed in remorse with his butt against the counter. "Booth will kill me."

"Not till he finds out."

"He's in town. He'll know any minute, I suspect."

"Where is he?"

"You looking for me, mister?"

Slocum turned and saw the red kerchief around the neck of the figure in the doorway. "We were just discussing you not a minute ago."

"No—no, we weren't—I mean, really, we weren't—" The youth tried to slip sideways toward the door to the back storeroom.

"He's ordering you some new guns. I'm taking these." Slocum gave the box a kick.

"Them's mine."

"In Campo, cash talks. Yours are on order."

Booth's eyes narrowed. "I'm getting gawdamn tired of you whoever you are."

"Maybe that's mutual."

"You're the one ran off my hands naked?"

"You lose some hands?"

Booth didn't answer, and moved his feet apart with a

jingle of his spurs, filling the doorway. "What's your name?"

"Slocum."

Booth nodded as if he recognized him. "We met once in San Saba."

At the mention of the town, Slocum recalled their previous brush. "You were working for Henry Tye?"

"Dumb Henry," Booth said, and shook his head. "You were working for that gal Lucy McCoy. Yeah, you kinda ran us boys off and hung Henry out to dry."

"You better think about this. You better pack up those cattle and go home."

Booth shook his head. "I'm taking over that range. It ain't under fence. It's free range."

"It won't be free."

The clerk, no longer able to stand it, rushed out the back entrance and the back door slammed. They were alone. Two men both armed. Both ready to draw.

"This ain't dumb Henry. The MC is a powerful outfit. Why, they could buy off enough New Mexico legislators to change the law."

"Except the federal judge recognized the grant."

"What's he going to do? Send that stupid greaser deputy out to scold us?" Booth began to laugh aloud.

His laughter was cut short and his knees buckled when Jeminez bashed him over the head with his pistol butt. Standing over him, he looked at Slocum. "I have got the packhorse."

"He have any more men out there?"

"Two."

"What did you do with them?" Slocum asked, picking up the boxes of ammo.

"They're in the stables, tied up. And I told them next time I caught them, I'd cut their nuts out."

"Bet they liked that." He picked up his side of the rifle case by the rope handle.

Jeminez took the other end of the box and shook his head. "Guess you had your chance to tell Booth he was fair game."

"I think after tonight he knows it."

Jeminez spit on his still form when he stepped over him. If not, he'd know soon enough.

Slocum bent over, jerked Booth's Colt out of his holster, and stuck it in his waistband. "Pays to defang rattlers."

Jeminez nodded. "I have the gun belts of the other two."

They strapped the case on top of the packsaddle and put the ammo in the pannier. At the sound of a moan, Slocum looked back. Booth was sitting up rubbing his head.

"You sonabitches are going to pay for this—"

In a flash, Jeminez was over him kicking the fire out of him. "This is for the boy and what you did to him."

The fury of the man kicking him had Booth desperately crawling away to escape the ruthless attack. Through his teeth Jeminez said, "I get you in my gun sight you're dead, hombre. Dead."

Hugging his sides, Booth began to holler, "Quit! Quit!"

Slocum forced Jeminez to stop and held him back. "He has the message or he's a helluva lot dumber than I think he is."

Jeminez, still enraged, tried to get by Slocum to get at Booth. "You want more, come for it. I have a .50-caliber Sharps that will end this."

They mounted their horses and leading the packhorse, headed out of the small settlement. Slocum looked back at the village, dark save for a few lights. They'd taken the war to the enemy. *What would the enemy do next?*

9

The sound of rifle shots whined in an echo across the draw. The men with rifles were having target practice. Jeminez was giving them instructions in Spanish.

"Shoot their horses, anything. I know it hurts to kill a good horse, but a Texan on foot is less dangerous and easier to shoot down than one on horseback. Aim. Don't close your eyes. That rifle won't hurt you going off.

"Load a shell in the chamber. Take aim slow, like he was coming at you, and then fire."

The report of the seven rifles was deafening and the black powder smoke went over them in the wind. Several men nodded in approval.

"Now go see where you hit. Was it where you aimed?"

Six of the seven had drilled holes in the boards set up for them. Jeminez nodded his approval. Then he put his arm over Alejandro's shoulder. "Did you close your eyes?"

"Ah, *sí*. I hate the loud shots." The shorter man shook his head.

"You know, in the cemetery you won't hear anything."

"Ah, *sí, amigo,* but—"

"Keep your eyes open and shoot that board."

"*Sí.*"

The others all stood back. Alejandro aimed and squeezed off a shot. A cheer went up and they clapped him on the back. "You did it."

"Clean your rifles now. Unload them. Unload them," Jeminez warned them as they moved off.

"You never thought they'd do this," Slocum said joining him.

"They are still a long ways from soldiers."

Slocum agreed, and the two men headed for the house and a siesta. After washing up, they went inside. The women were putting food on the table.

"Well?" Belle asked, carrying the kettle of beans with both hands on the handle.

"They all can hit a large board," Slocum said.

"I would give anything to know what Booth is doing." Jeminez took off his sombrero and sat down in the straight-back chair.

"Trying to heal after the kicking you gave him. Pass the tortillas."

"I hope he never heals. My toes still hurt."

"The men can guard the ranch. Let's start the MC cattle eastward. We can start in the north and work this way."

"Who will go?"

"Belle's ready," Slocum said, and grinned over at her. "I think her, two more drovers, and myself. You can be our point man with the Sharps."

"I'm ready," she said.

Jeminez looked hard at him. "I am going to shoot to kill."

"Your call. We've probably reached that point." His plans to deter the Texans hadn't been a total success. The notion of an all-out war left him concerned, but he also didn't know what else they could do. The MC had made their bed. They could lie in it.

After lunch, Slocum and Belle headed for the barn and their bed for a siesta. There was silence between them as he toed off his boots. She chewed on her lower lip.

"This gets very serious from here on, doesn't it? This range war business?"

"Very serious." He took off his gun belt and glanced across at her. She was undoing the buttons down the front of her dress. He stepped over and stood before her. "Sorry I got you into this—I know we were on the way to find Wesley Harrigan."

She hugged him. "I know I've used you." Her forehead against his chest, she continued. "But after they shot Hank, I had no one. When I'm in your arms, I forget. Forget Harrigan. Forget Hank even."

He used his fist to raise her chin up and kissed her. "That's what I'm for."

Her arms grew tighter around him. "Then let's forget."

He pulled her dress open as she fumbled with his shirt buttons. His hands cupped her pear-shaped breasts and his thumb teased the right nipple into hardening as their mouths sought each other. The garment slid off her shoulders and he lost his pants. She stripped the shirt off him and then bounced her butt on the bed with a beckoning look.

He shed his socks and was on his knees crawling to where she sprawled on her back in the center of the bed. The flickering shadowy light from the two open windows shone on her ripe body as the wind outside tossed the cottonwoods. He moved between her raised knees and smiled down on her.

Her fingers reached down, clutched him by the shaft, and she raised her butt and inserted him in her gates. His own butt ached to probe her. He eased into her depth and began to drive himself in and out. Her eyes closed and she raised her chin and uttered, "Yes."

Braced over her, he worked against her muscular walls, which began to contract. Their breath grew shorter from the effort. Her stiff clit was scratching the top of his dick like a sharp stick and only added to their excitement. He went deeper and harder and faster. They became a tornado with his skintight dick in the middle of the vortex and the bed ropes screaming in protest. They kissed without missing a beat, and they gasped for their breath as the ocean they rode tossed and turned.

He felt two hot needles pierce the cheeks of his ass and he plunged deeper inside her. Their pubic bones mashed together. His testicles cramped with the explosion inside them and the hot cum flew out the head of his swollen dick. She fainted.

Like a drunk, she opened her glazed eyes and looked up at him braced over her. "I told you I forgot every—thing."

"Good."

They slept for a few hours in each other's arms.

In the late afternoon, he reset the shoes on his horse. Bent over and feeling the tight muscles in his back, he used the rasp to cut down the hoof, shedding gray shavings off on the ground as he shaped it. He dropped the hoof and looked at his handiwork.

"Is it sitting flat?" he asked Belle as she sat on a keg and observed him.

"Not bad. You always shoe your own?"

"When I can't afford a farrier."

"You broke?"

"No, only kidding. I have money. I just wanted this done before we go after those cattle. Your horse looks fine." He went back to tacking on the shoe.

"When this is all over, where will you go?"

"On down the road."

She shook her head and smiled. "You get into fixes like this a lot?"

"I don't know about a lot. But folks sometimes need help."

"There is no money here. Why, you could join the MC and get top wages."

Bent over, he took the horseshoe nails out of his mouth. "I ain't run off any settlers in my life for hire."

She nodded that she understood. "Guess I read that about you the first time we met. I was just curious."

"Those fellas on my back trail could show up any day." He released the hoof and admired his handiwork. It looked good enough. He had three more to go.

"What then?"

"I'd have to move on."

"Why not face them down?"

He laughed on the other side of the horse with its hoof in his lap. "Then they might send someone that could catch me."

They both laughed.

It was early when they awoke the next morning. They hadn't slept much the night before with their lovemaking and the tussling they did in bed. He threw his legs over the side of the bed, rubbed his beard stubble in his calloused hands, and tried to open his eyes.

He felt her firm breast buried in his back as she hugged him possessively from behind. "We're going to let off a volley today, aren't we?"

"When they get the notion that we're serious, I expect we will."

"Oh, why can't we stay here and do this all day?" She rocked him back and forth.

"'Cause—'cause we need to solve this MC problem and head for Texas."

She kissed his ear. "What sort of man is this Harrigan, do you think?"

"He's a bounty hunter. He's tough as rawhide and don't give any quarter."

"I won't ever forget my ordeal in the outhouse. I look every time I open the door to one expecting to find someone concealed in there."

His pants on, he sat back down, bent over, and pulled on a boot. "That too will go away in time."

"Like you will?"

"Not till I have to."

She put the shirt on and buttoned it. He put on his holster and watched her long legs slide in the overalls as she lay back to pull them up and close the fly. Maybe he could push a good-sized herd eastward—the day would tell.

Garmo and Rojo were the two boys sent along. Garmo was a big boy for his fifteen years and fat, but he sat his horse good. The second helper was younger, smaller, and had reddish hair; he looked like a natural horseman. They took along a packhorse with bedrolls, some horse grain, and a minimum of food. Jerky, a cornmeal-sugar mixture, some dried fruit, dry cheese, and crackers. In the early morning they rode out to the quiet cheers of the families. Jeminez told Raul to have guards and lookouts ready all the time while they were gone.

In an hour the small party had over a hundred head of steers in a bunch headed east. Slocum didn't expect to find this many that fast. Obviously the MC had been pushing them harder on to the ranch land than he'd imagined. Belle rode swing on the left and Rojo on the right. He and Garmo kept the herd moving and fought the stragglers to make them keep up. No sign of Jeminez, who was scouting ahead. Slocum knew the cloud of dust they were boiling up would give notice if anyone was looking.

At midday Belle came back on the fly. "Shots ahead. I heard some."

Slocum jerked down the bandanna over his face to filter the dust. "Circle the herd. I'll go see what I can do."

He set his horse off in a hard gallop for the east and past the herd. Heading for some high ground, he took out his field glasses as he rode with the wind in his face. On the rise, he set the pony down and began to scan the country to his east.

Jeminez had captured one cowboy, who had his hands in the air, and the other was lying on the ground. Their horses were close by, as well as a good bunch of steers they must have been herding west. Slocum looked for any sign of more. Nothing. Putting his glasses in his saddlebags, he swung up and galloped for Jeminez.

"You get two of them?" he asked as he pulled up and slipped off his horse.

"He went for his gun when I fired the first shot at them."

Slocum nodded and looked at the youth who was still alive. He was close to tears and trembling so bad his teeth were chattering.

"Who are you?"

"Na-Nash Cobble."

"Where's your momma?"

"Coleman County."

Slocum looked him hard in the eye. "If we let you go, can you get on that horse and ride straight there?"

"I-I s-sure kin."

"Well, if you ever want to see her again, then you better skip that MC camp and keep on trotting till you get home. You savvy? 'Cause the next time there won't be no going home."

"I-I understand."

"What's Booth doing?"

"Ah, he's laid up in camp. Got some broke ribs. Some fellas gave him a helluva beating."

Slocum shared a nod of approval with Jeminez. "Load your butt on that horse and get out of here."

"Ah, yes, sir." He swept up his hat and ran for the cow pony, who jerked its head up with grass in the bit. "Don't shoot me, please—"

"Go back to MC camp, you're a dead man." Slocum cupped his hands around his mouth to deliver the message.

"I won't—" And whipping the horse, he raced south.

Slocum could see the other one was dead. The .50-caliber

hole in his chest had ended his life. An older man, he looked in his thirties, and Slocum did not recognize him as someone he knew or had seen. Just one more drover who bit the dust.

"What do we do now?" Jeminez asked.

"We drive these and all the cattle we have back there east the rest of the day, then stampede them toward Texas."

"What about him?"

"All we can do is cave in a bank on him. We didn't bring a shovel."

Jeminez agreed and pointed out a place to bury him. They loaded him belly-down over his horse and led him across to the wash. Using their rifle butts for shovels, they soon had him buried under the loose dirt. Slocum found a pencil and paper. He tied a note on the saddle string. *Quit and go home or die,* it said. Then he took the bridle off and slapped the horse on the butt with the reins. It tucked its tail and tore out for the east.

Slocum sent Jeminez ahead to clear the way and rode back to the herd. He had two six-guns in holsters from the two MC hands. More guns and ammo in case they needed it. They soon had the herd moving and were adding to it.

Slocum figured they had close to three hundred head on the move. It was going to be a great event if they could stampede them east.

"What happened?" Belle asked when he rode up to check on her.

He shook his head. "You don't want to know."

"Fine," she said, and shook her head. "We making good time?"

"The way these steers are moving, they'll be well off the ranch's land by dark."

"Really?"

"Yeah, they'll lose some weight, but who cares. Keep them rolling," he said, and left her to hurry back and help Garmo. It was one thing to push cattle ten to twelve miles a day on a drive and then let them graze all afternoon, but at a steady trot they could cover three to four miles an hour— eight to ten hours would put them well off the ranch's range.

By the time sundown set the western sky afire, they had well over five hundred head on the run. So when Slocum started firing his pistol in the air, they fled, and their thundering hooves going off into the twilight drew smiles on the riders' dusty faces.

"We had a good day," Belle said.

"Wonderful one. I figure the MC tally has over two thousand head up here, so we have lots more to run off."

"That many?" Garmo asked, fumbling with his wet latigos to unsaddle his horse.

"Could be more, but I'd bet that many."

"And we only had five hundred head of them bawling devils today?" Rojo asked.

"That wasn't a bad roundup for four of us."

"Whew, my seat's going to be sore before we get all of them," Rojo said.

Belle clapped him on the shoulder and passed out some jerky as Jeminez rode in.

"Any more trouble?" Slocum asked him.

"I saw two cowboys riding southwest, but I didn't have them in range. They weren't herding cattle either."

"I don't know how long we can keep making drives and not meet up with Booth."

Jeminez took a swig out of his canteen and gargled before he spit it out. "What do you think?"

"Go home tomorrow and rest a day and then start out of the south with another bunch."

Jeminez agreed. "I seen them running by. That was a big bunch you chased off the ranch."

"I figure five to six hundred head."

"Saved some of our grass, amigo."

Slocum agreed.

They woke up the next morning as a monsoon rain moved in. The boys had no slickers and used their blankets instead. A steady drizzle on light winds swept them all day. Distant thunder rolled over the land, and the precipitation lasted much longer than Slocum would have guessed—a good soaking rain. The kind stockmen dream about, and Jeminez was smiling all day.

When they rode in, they were mobbed by people asking questions about what they'd done. Slocum reined up his horses beside Jeminez.

"We sent many head of cattle back beyond our land and have many more to drive," Jeminez said.

"Any trouble?" someone asked.

He shook his head. "No trouble." And they pushed on.

Slocum looked back as they rounded the corner. "Reckon those two boys heard us talking?"

"They're good boys. I told them best the others did not know."

"Your call," Slocum said, and shared a nod with a serious-faced Belle. They were his people.

10

"There is law here," Belle whispered in his ear.

He raised up on his elbows. "What for?"

"They have a paper of some kind. A court order."

"What in the hell is that about?" He began to dress, and jerked on his boots in the room's darkness.

He nodded to Jeminez as he strapped on his holster while going by the front porch. "What's going on?"

There were lights on in Raul's house and three strange horses tied in front at the rack. Slocum let Jeminez go in first. After checking around and seeing nothing out of place, he also went inside.

A big man with an expensive hat and a walrus mustache turned around in a chair and looked at him hard, then glanced back to Jeminez.

"See, Don Jeminez, the sheriff has a court order that a judge has ruled your land grant is invalid."

"That's right," the so-called sheriff said. "That means you can't stop the grazing on this land until this is settled in court."

"You work for the MC?" Slocum asked.

The chair scraped on the tile and the big man rose. "I never caught your name."

"Tom White. A federal judge declared their grant as valid. Who is this judge?"

"Mr. White, I'm the law in this county and I enforce the law."

"Let me see that paper." Slocum took it from Raul. He looked down to the signature—JUSTICE OF THE PEACE SAMUEL DUGGER, LAS VEGAS, NMT. "This Dugger can't invalidate a federal court order, he's only a justice of the peace. His jurisdiction doesn't go all over the county either."

"Sheriff Garcia, are you going to enforce this court order or not?" the man with the small black mustache demanded.

"Since we're getting on a first-name basis, what's your name?" Slocum asked.

"Barton, Alex Barton of Barton, Schofeld, and Morris."

"And who are you?" Slocum asked the third man.

"Court clerk for Judge Dugger. Martin Goldstein. I am here to see the law is carried out."

"Barton's a lawyer for the MC, right?"

With his coat lapels in both hands, the lawyer stuck his chest out. "My firm represents many interests in the livestock business."

"No, the MC is footing the bill for you to come out here and that ain't cheap. And I suppose that Sheriff Garcia is going to issue deputy badges to every MC cowboy to enforce this worthless document."

Obviously affronted by Slocum's accusation, Garcia scowled at him. "I'll deputize anyone I see fit."

"All the MC crew or just the ones that aren't on wanted posters?"

Garcia frowned at Barton. Good, he'd hit a sore spot.

"I assure you that none of the MC employees are wanted men," Barton shot back at Slocum.

"When you go to their camp to make them deputies, better take along a stack of them bills. There's more faces over there on them than there are in Tascosa."

"I'll have you know—" Garcia blustered red-faced at him.

"Have me know what? That you were going to send a box of badges over there with Barton here and let him handle it? Was that what you were going to say?"

The sheriff pointed his finger at Slocum. "I am the law in the county—"

"Yes, and you sleep with this MC bunch and you won't be after the next election. Those Texans can't vote here."

Garcia pounded his fist on the table. "This is a valid court order."

"This is crap." Slocum reached over and tossed the paper at Goldstein, the court clerk. He fumbled to catch it, looking bug-eyed at Slocum. "You tell your boss to stick with sentencing drunks to thirty days. He has no authority to challenge a federal decree."

"I am placing you under arrest for blocking a court order."

Slocum shook his head like that was impossible. "I don't think you noticed. There are several rifle barrels at each window. I'd hate to attend your funeral."

"This is insurrection!"

"Sheriff, Sheriff," Barton said with his hand on the man's arm to restrain him. "I think we can handle this matter in Superior Court."

"No one is going to tell me—you're under arrest in the name of the Territory of New Mexico."

The metallic click of rifles being cocked was the loudest sound in the predawn. Garcia's eyes turned to slits. Then, glaring at Slocum, he dried his palms on his fancy woolen pants. Barton was dragging him to the doorway. Goldstein was like a panicked sheep trying to get in between them as they hurried outside.

"You better not go against that order," Gracia shouted from horseback, and the threesome left like foxes with hounds on their butts headed south.

"Is what you said for sure the truth?" Raul asked.

Slocum nodded, watching them retreat. "It was just a

deal they thought they could slap down and you'd be so afraid you'd believe it."

"I would never have known better," Jeminez said. "I can't read that good."

"A lawyer would have laughed at it," Slocum said. "They aren't through. They're going to try every trick in the book and you better believe me they have more."

"What can we do?" Raul asked.

"Guard the ranch from raids and send four more men with us today. While they are licking their wounds, I want to push more cattle east."

Slocum's teeth were about ready to float out for some coffee, but he stopped and turned to the men and women gathered in the square. "You have done a brave thing this morning. They will try and try over and over again to take your ranchero. But we can win. We started really winning today."

Jeminez nodded at his words and they went to the house. Belle rushed out and before she could even speak, he caught her upper arms and kissed her hard on the mouth. He could taste the honey in her mouth, and her firm body against him felt exciting. Hank Nelson must have been a real man—shame he never met him. Bigger shame she and Hank couldn't have lived out their dreams on the ranch they were building. Finally he hugged her. "You know we've got cattle to move today?"

She swept the hair back from her face. "Yes, and we have breakfast ready."

"Ah, Slocum ran off the lawyers and the sheriff today," Jeminez said as Juanita came out to see what was keeping them.

"Good. Come in and eat before it gets cold."

Slocum looked at the eastern sky where the purple of dawn began to crease the horizon. *What would the Texans try next?*

11

The rain had settled the dust, but the cattle were more scattered since they didn't need to walk back to a water source with pools in every dry wash or depression. But the additional riders helped them cover more ground making a large sweep, and cattle soon came pouring in from all directions. They also had to cut out the cattle bearing the brand of the Rancho de Vaca. Since its animals had been herded in that direction, there were many in the herd that they assembled at midday.

Ropes and reatas sliced the air. Ropers rode amongst the cattle to catch the ones who were not the MC's. Bawling cows and even some calves were dragged out of the large herd and sent away by three young boys who rode out to help.

Slocum decided there was no way they'd do more than finish culling before the day was gone, and sent word to Raul via a youth helping them. His crew would need food and blankets so they could hold the cattle in a bunch overnight and start east with them in the morning.

"How many do we have?" Belle asked him when he rode to where she sat her horse.

"We'll have five hundred or more when we get through."

"They really have been pushing their cattle on here, haven't they?"

Slocum agreed. "More than I even imagined. This many head, they'd've eaten up the ranch's range in a short while."

"Now what?" She used the back of her glove to push an errant wave of hair back toward her hat.

"I sent for food and blankets. We'll spend the night here and then trot this bunch hard east."

She winked at him. "Save a place in your bedroll for me."

He looked off across the sea of grass at a small mesa with black volcanic rock sides. "Wish I was an eagle, could see what they're doing."

"Why not take your glasses and go up there and look?" she said, indicating the rise.

"Might work. I'll go tell Don Jeminez he's in charge. You want to go along? They about have the ranch cattle cut out."

"Sure, why not?"

After putting Jeminez in charge, they raced across the open ground, spooking cottontails and jacks. At the base of the mesa, he loosened cinches and hobbled the horses. She took a blanket roll and retrieved his field glasses from the saddlebags.

Slocum studied the sheer wall searching for a way up it. Then, with his eyes squinted against the sun, he thought he saw a possible route.

"Let's go," he said, shouldering the blanket roll.

She smiled and, holding a canteen and with field glass around her neck, she joined him. He led the way and glanced back as he strove to climb the steep wall. Right behind him she came grinning. His breath became short from real exertion in places, and he reached back several times to haul her up with him, until at last they topped the grassy flat. He unfurled the blanket, then bellied down to search the far-flung plains dotted with an occasional juniper.

She joined him and handed him the field glasses. He scanned the country to the east for any sign of activity.

"See anything?" she asked.

He shook his head. The MC crew was out there brewing up something. If only he knew their plans and could nip them off. But there was no way, he'd have to face them as they came to him. Another drive after this one would mean more time sorting out ranch cattle mixed with the MC herd. But another drive might clear them all off the ranch.

What would happen then? He glanced over. She was lying on her back looking whimsically out from under her hat brim. "What were you thinking?" he asked.

She rolled over to face him and propped her head up on an elbow. "What I usually think when I am in bed with you."

"Oh."

"Oh, my foot. You realize how little time we've had to be alone?"

He turned over on his back and studied the clear azure sky. "No, but if you think I've given up on you, you're wrong."

"Good." She bolted up and began unbuttoning her blouse. "Show me."

He laughed, sitting up and jerking off his boots. "Lady, you ever been seduced on a mesa top before?"

She paused, ready to pull the shirt back, and looked reflectively at him. "No, I can't recall that ever happening."

He was on his knees, unbuckling his gun belt and laughing. "Today is the day."

"Wonderful," she said, and scrambled to her feet. She shed her britches, and the sun shone on snowy legs that led to a shapely derriere. With her shirt off at last, her proud breasts shook at him like the tempting apples of Eden. In desperation to get to her, he fought off his underwear and tackled her. They landed on the blanket, and he pushed the hair from her face to find her mouth.

In each other's clutches, their lips mashed hard together. Then he worked his way over her legs and once he was between them, she raised her knees. His urge to drive his throbbing dick in her was inflamed, and he pushed forward in an attempt to plunge through her gates.

She reached under him and set it on course. Then she settled on her back at his entry, and gasped at the passage of his enlarged erection through her tight ring. It was slick enough with her natural lubricant, but he still felt the muscled constriction and it required a full thrust to pump into her.

Braced on top of her, he smiled down as he threw himself into it. Again and again his thrust sought her depths—her clit scraping the top of his rock-hard pecker like a large nail. With her heels locked behind his knees, she too fought the war and raised her butt off the blanket to meet his actions. Harder, faster, more, more. Every nerve in the length of his sore swollen dick was electrified by the friction of her contracting walls and the sensations that led to the finale.

"Oh," came from her parted lips as she tossed her head from side to side deliriously in pleasure's arms. Her hard stomach pressed against the cords of muscles that rippled down his belly. Like a fiery torch, the swollen head of his dick screamed for relief, plunging in and out of the swollen tunnel until, at last out of breath, he halted braced above her. Dizzy and fearing the task had no end, he raised his sweaty face up to let the wind cool it.

Then, with a newfound fury, he attacked her harder than ever before. His surges were stronger, more deliberate, with longer strokes, until they both were lost in a desperate whirlwind that drew from the depths of his balls molten-hot lava. It erupted out of the head, and she cried out in stiffening surrender under his onslaught. Her sharp nails dug into the muscles of his upper arms until she collapsed in a heap beneath him.

They slept in each other's arms until a screaming redtailed hawk challenged their presence on his range. Slocum fought to open his eyes in the glare and see it as its shadow passed over them. Grinning at the bird of prey's loud insistence, he sat up, and she hugged his arm to keep him there.

He smiled at her, then rolled over and used the glasses. They had company coming. "We better get down there."

"What's the matter?" she asked, busy dressing.

"Three, four, five riders are coming from the east. They're Texans by their hats, and I'd say they have rifles."

"What can we do?"

"I'll try and stop them."

"Not without me."

"Too dangerous."

She pulled him half up to stare hard in his face. "I'm going with you."

He put down the glass. "Then we better get our butts off this mesa and head them off."

In minutes, they were dressed and scrambling down the mountainside for their grazing horses. With the hobbles off, and cinches tightened, they swung in their saddles, jerking rifles out of their scabbards as they set in a hard run for the east. Those riders were taking a wagon road and he hoped to waylay them.

Meadowlarks, quail, and jackrabbits fled aside at their hard approach. On top of the rise, they paralleled the wagon tracks on a ridge headed for the jumble of juniper and rocks where he hoped to ambush the riders.

They dismounted from their hard-breathing horses in a wash, and he hitched them to a small cottonwood and told her to follow him up the steep slope. The steep climb had them out of breath, but crouched in a nest of boulders, he felt they had won the race as he checked the chamber of his .44/40. Satisfied it was loaded, he sat back and listened.

"You believe that hawk warned us?"

He looked over at her, hearing the drum of hooves, and slowly nodded. "They're coming. I don't want them killed if they'll surrender, but if their guns come out, then we need to put them down."

She nodded and bit her lip.

"It's their decision."

"Yes," she said quietly, and took off her hat. With her hands, she swept her hair back and tied it with a ribbon. "I'm ready."

The snort of the oncoming horses and steel shoes striking rocks drew closer; then the men's voices began to carry to Slocum's hideout. Rifle ready, he rose and aimed it at them in the narrow confines of the draw.

"Throw down your arms!"

"What in the hell—"

"Drop 'em or die!"

One of the riders jerked his horse around and went for his sidearm. Slocum's Winchester blasted him out of the saddle. An acrid sweep of black powder washed over his face, with his cheek hard pressed on the polished stock, and he levered in another cartridge. Ready for another to try something.

The cowboys halted their ponies and shouted, "Don't shoot."

"Cover me," he said to her and she nodded, holding the rifle to her shoulder and ready for anything. "Get off them ponies and put your hands up high. Step away from them."

On his boot heels, he slid down the slope and with the rifle ready, he circled them making certain they had no other arms that he could detect.

"We're just drovers, mister," one of them said.

"Where's Booth?"

"In camp, I guess. He can't ride. They busted his ribs in a fight."

"What were your orders?"

"Check on the cattle."

"Five of you together?"

"Well—to see if any of them greasers was rounding up our stock."

"What then?"

The older one doing the talking shrugged. "I guess stop them."

"Like some of you beat up that boy with the sheep?"

The man held out his hands as if to ward off the accusation. "Wasn't us—"

"Oh, no, but you'd've done it today. The boss said for you to, didn't he?"

The man swallowed hard, and the rest of the punchers shared worried looks.

"Mister, you give us a chance, we'll quit this outfit and ride out of here."

"Put your arms down. How many punchers are left besides you four?"

"None. There's a cook, a kid helps him, and two gunhands not counting Booth."

"Where are those gunhands?"

"In camp—resting," the kid of the bunch said. "Everyone else besides us quit. Booth's sending for more if the supply wagons ever get here."

"It's late?" Slocum asked, concealing his amusement.

"Them wagons should have been here by now."

"You boys promise to ride for the Big Bend country, I might consider giving you a pardon. If you go back and join Booth, I won't tell you to halt next time. I'll gun you down."

Seriousness masked their somber faces—heads nodded.

"What about Hoot?" One of the others nodded toward the one lying crumpled on the ground.

"Shame he didn't listen. Load him up and somewhere you can borrow a shovel and plant him."

"We'll do that."

"Just remember this is your final chance. Join Booth and you'll die with him."

"Them greasers paying you a lot?" the kid asked, trying to get on his shying horse.

Slocum shook his head. "Some old friends I owed a favor to."

"They better be damn grateful they got you. Booth's got a big rep for cleaning out ranges of anyone gets in his way. Guess he never met the likes of you before." The kid finally mounted his horse and checked him so he could look back for Slocum's reply.

"He did once with me and lost."

The kid's shoulder shook with his silent amusement. "Hell, he never told us that."

"Mister," the older one said. "Could I ask your name?"

"Slocum."

The man shook his head like he'd never heard it before. "You and I get on cross sides again, just tell me it's you and I'll join yeah or ride on."

"Ride on," Slocum said, and they led the dead one belly-down over his horse.

If they recognized Belle as a woman, they never made mention. She'd tucked her hair under her hat before she came down, and stayed well above them, holding the rifle ready. When they filed away, Slocum scrambled up to where she stood.

"There's only three left in that camp. That's counting Booth. Guess Jeminez and I better see about them."

"What did they say about Booth?"

"He's got some broken ribs that Jeminez caved in when he kicked him. He's too sore to ride."

"Those were the last MC hands?"

"That's what they said. Booth plans on sending word back by the supply wagons for more help."

She looked at him hard. "They're not coming."

"No way. We know that."

"Back to the herd?"

He agreed, and they went for their horses.

In the red-orange light of sundown, they rode into the setup camp and Raul came to meet them. His face was lined with concern, and he looked sleepless and filled with questions.

"What have you learned?"

Slocum dismounted. "We ran off the last cowboys today. There are only three gunhands in their camp. One's Booth, and he's got broken ribs and it hurts him too much to ride."

"What about all these cattle?" Raul indicated the herd that was bedded down south of them.

"We need to take them past the east side of your range. Send along some supplies, spare horses, so we can drive them hard for a few days."

"Do we have all of them?"

"All but a few hundred head, I figure. Those left you can gather and drive to the stockyards at the railroad, give them to the brand inspector as strays, and he can ship them."

"The people of the Rancho owe you much. I would never have challenged that law business. These people have risen as our ancestors would have done when they were challenged, but only because of you."

"No, Don Jeminez did much of this."

"Yes."

"Where is he?" Belle asked, looking around for him as a woman brought them food on trays.

"He has not been seen all day, Señora," the woman said.

"I better go look for him," Slocum said.

Belle laid a hand on his arm. "Soon it will be dark and how could you find him?"

Slocum agreed, though Jeminez not being back niggled at him. With each bite of the rich spicy food, he wondered where his friend was and why he hadn't returned. Despite the mouth-watering flavor, the food became harder to swallow. Somewhere a coyote yelped and Slocum listened—no sounds of anyone returning in the night.

12

He had both their horses saddled before the first glimpse of sunrise appeared over the wide horizon. Nowhere in the West was the face of dawn wider than on the plains. From Canada to the Rio Grande, the sky took up more of one's vision than in any place he'd ever been. There were places in this region where everything looked like it was downhill from where a person stood. Slocum had heard about the poles on the top and bottom of the earth, but for him the top of the earth was somewhere on this strip of land.

He put feed bags on the horses, left them crunching corn, and went to join Belle at the campfire. She handed him a plate of food and a fork. "Don Jeminez never came in?"

He shook his head. "That's not like him."

"Where will we start looking?"

"East and north of where we were yesterday. His mule should be easy to track, he's shod."

"You think something happened to him?"

"Strange he never came in. I can't imagine."

"Señor," Raul said to him. "Should we move the cattle today?"

"Yes, put your best riflemen out ahead. One on each side, and use the boys that drove the other bunch as swing riders. Once you get them headed east, have the swing riders move in closer until they are trotting and keep up the pace. You should make thirty—thirty-five miles and then bed them down. The next day do the same, then stampede them."

"But how will the women and *carretas* keep up to make camp?"

"They will have to hurry all day to catch up later. Since the next day will be the last day and the cattle will be stampeded, the women can stop halfway and make camp. The drovers can come back to them that evening."

"Ah, *sí*. We will do it as you say."

"We'll find Don Jeminez and we'll be along to help."

"Señor, be careful. We owe you so much. How will we ever pay you?"

"You don't owe me anything but a place to hang my hat when I ride through. But the MC outfit won't take this lying down. You have shown them what you can do. I fear they won't like it."

"*Sí*, I savvy. But after this my people will be stronger and they will learn the edge of our knife is sharp."

"It will have to be. Time to ride, Belle," he said to her, and shook Raul's hand.

With the feed bags off and cinches tightened, they left the cluster of well-wishers and rode eastward.

"Spread out," he said, standing in the stirrups and trotting. "A mule shoe is long and narrow where a horse's shoe is more circular."

She nodded and swung to the side, searching the ground. After a quarter mile she shouted, "Over here."

He loped his pony over and, at the sight of the tracks, agreed with a grin. "That's Tonto's, all right."

They moved against the fresh sun that bathed the land in a golden glare. Meadowlarks and plovers raced ahead at their approach. The land they crossed proved to be rolling, with some deeper draws, and he scouted them from the rims, looking for any sign. Nothing but the mule's hoof-prints in the soft dirt that guided them.

They spooked up a small pocket of a half-dozen MC cattle that ran away like deer. It would take a couple of roundups to clear the range of the Texas cattle. Some of those old brush cutters had hidden from capture for most of their lives in the thick mesquite thickets of south Texas. They'd be as hard to catch again as they had been originally. Folks called them *haints*.

He rode the left side, with her on the right edge of the long hogback, both searching the steep grassy slopes for any sign. A large buck deer rose from his bed in a low cluster of mesquite. One look over his shoulder and, with his ten-point rack held high, he bounded away.

"Slocum," she called out. "I see his mule and think he's under it."

Slocum charged over and reined up his horse on the brink. Far down the hillside, the red mule was lying on his side not moving. Slocum never hesitated, and sent the horse down off the brink. On his hind hooves the pony skidded downhill, on his butt most of the way. Slocum jumped off before the animal stopped, and ran over to the mule.

"Don Jeminez. Don Jeminez. You all right?" He dropped on his knees beside the still-hatless body pinned under the dead mule.

A black bloody bullet wound behind the mule's front leg told part of the story. When the mule went down, he'd pinned Jeminez underneath. The .50-caliber Sharps lay a few feet away.

"Is he shot?"

Slocum shook his head. "I don't know—"

His finger sought a pulse behind his friend's ear. Nothing. He dropped to his butt and closed his eyes. Don Jeminez wouldn't ever answer him. His buffalo-hunting partner was gone.

"What's wrong—"

"He's dead." Slocum swept off his hat and stood up. Could he have found and saved his friend the night before? No way they would have ever found him in the darkness. Slocum dreaded worst of all having to tell Juanita.

"Juanita," rolled off Belle's lips at the same moment.

Slocum nodded.

"Was he shot?"

"No, but the mule was shot. I'll tie a rope on the saddle and we'll pull the mule off him."

She nodded, biting her lower lip, and then ran for her horse. He took the rope off Jeminez's saddle and tied it around the hull, then took the end to Belle's in the saddle. She dallied it around the horn and Slocum rushed back to help push. The rope grew tight and she put spurs to her pony. The mule's body began to slide away as Slocum pushed on it with both hands to help. In the confines of the steep slopes, they finally managed to get Tonto clear of the limp body.

She bounded off her horse and picked up the Sharps. Then she ran over to him. "Was he shot?"

"I can't see any marks. Unless he hit his head on a rock when the mule went down, I guess we'll never know." He picked the man up in his arms and carried him to her horse. "We need to take him home."

Her grim face set, she nodded and hurried around to the far side. "Tie him on?"

"Yes, I'll get the lariat off the saddle." He slid the body over the seat and then hurried downhill for the rope. As he picked his way, he couldn't swallow the knot behind his tongue. Damn, who'd shot the mule? Some of the MC bunch—no doubt. Slocum had no time to scout the area or even search for a shell casing or tracks.

He started back with the lariat and saw someone on the ridge. "Belle, get down."

She whirled and then dove for the ground. The black smoke of the gunshot appeared on the hill as, like an angry

hornet, the bullet cut the air close by Slocum; then came
the crack of the rifle as he scrambled for the Sharps. Another shot echoed in the confines of the draw. He noted that
Belle had hidden behind a rock outcropping.

He picked up the rifle and dove sideways. In the cover
of the wash's overhang, he opened the chamber and noted
the cartridge. Easing the rifle's works back, he swung the
muzzle around hoping it had not been jarred in the fall. Hot
chips of rock stung the side of his face as another bullet
ricocheted close by.

"Keep down," he said to Belle, grateful she was behind
better protection than he was. The next shot sent dirt at him
when the bullet struck to his left. He rose and caught the
distant figure in his sight. His finger squeezed off the trigger, and the heavy rifle slammed into his shoulder like a
mule kicking him. He'd forgotten the recoil of one of these
cannons. He dropped down again.

"You hit him!"

Gun smoke stung his eyes as he rose and tried to clear
them to see. The horse was gone and no one was in sight on
the ridge. No time to take chances. He rushed over to Jeminez's body, which had fallen off when the shots spooked
their horses. He found six more shells in his friend's
pocket. With the long brass cartridges in his hand, he reloaded the Sharps and then started uphill.

"Be careful," Belle said after him.

"You stay hidden till I tell you it's clear."

The climb up the hill proved hard, with Slocum checking the rim every few seconds, expecting the shooter to be
looking down the barrel of his rifle at him. Slocum's footing slipped in places on loose rocks as he went up the steep
slope.

Out of breath, he reached the top, spotting the nearby
horse and the man facedown. With his hard gaze on the still
ambusher, Slocum knelt, laid the rifle down, and drew his
Colt. He moved to the man and studied him. Then, with the

.44 back in the holster, he squatted on his heels and lifted the body to turn it over. The shooter's vest was a bloody mess. The man's gray eyes stared at eternity. He was in his thirties, with a full mustache and a bad scar under his right eye. Slocum'd never seen this one before. Must work for the MC. Nothing else in sight but the bay horse. Had this dry-gulcher watched for them using Jeminez's body as the bait? He'd never know. Weary from all the hurrying around, Slocum rose and went to the rim.

"He's dead too," he shouted to Belle. "I'm coming."

She nodded and hurried down the ravine to get their animals.

They both worked to load Jeminez's corpse over her horse and tied it down. She rode Slocum's horse, and led them both down the draw to circle back up on the rim. He went directly up the hill, caught the MC-branded horse and loaded the dead man on it. Besides the man's expensive custom-made sniper rifle, Slocum, found a sweat stained letter addressed to Tom Burks.

"Find out who he was?" Belle reined up before him as he read the paper.

"Burks—never heard of him. Says here his father wasn't expected to live. Been bitten by a snake in the granary."

"Guess Burks should have gone to see him," she said.

Slocum nodded at her. "And now there are two left."

"Where was he hiding when we rode up?"

"I'm not sure. But he obviously made Don Jeminez the bait. He'd been a little better shot, he'd've had us. We can ride my horse double and lead these others."

"Fine. We going by the herd?"

"Not unless they're in the way going back. Bodies in this heat will swell fast. I want Don Jeminez buried this afternoon."

"I understand. Then what?"

"I'm going to find Booth and send him to hell." He swung her up and she said, "Yes."

Making a seat behind him, she hugged him tight and laid her face on his back. "You're a tough man, Slocum."

"Not tough enough to protect my friends."

"Don Jeminez knew what he was doing."

"I should have been here."

"He never expected you to."

That still didn't settle it for him. Slocum reached out and caught the other rein. Both horses in tow, he set his pony in a long lope for the ranch. It would be late afternoon before they ever arrived there. Grim job—one he hated to even think about. But as he rode in the rocking gait with her holding on tight to him, he decided it wasn't all bad.

They missed the herd, seeing the dust in the south, and rode on to the ranch. The horse was tired, dropping his head in the dust when they arrived at Juanita's doorstep. Juanita ran out drying her hands. From the look on her face, she knew full well the corpse over the horse was her husband.

Her cries of anguish carried in the last hour of daylight with the sun sinking fast. Belle slid off and rushed over to hug her. Juanita's sorrow drew others to come on the run. Someone rang the church bell, and more of the anxious ranch people came running.

"How did he meet his death?"

"Was this other one his killer?"

The questions filled the air as Slocum carried his friend inside. The priest's assistant came with a Bible to read over him. Women fell on their knees to clasp their hands in the air and pray, concerned about their own men driving the cattle. Slocum laid the body on the floor on a blanket Juanita and Belle spread for him.

"Did they shoot him?" Juanita asked.

Slocum shook his head. "He either hit his head in the fall or had a heart seizure. They shot Tonto. I don't know, there are no bullet wounds I could find."

Wet-eyed, she nodded at Slocum. "I know he appreciated what you did for these people."

"He would have done as much for me. I will see about graves."

"No," a man who seemed to be in charge said. "The graves are being dug at this minute. The boys are putting up your horses."

Slocum slumped against the wall. A small gray-haired woman shoved a cup into his hand. "Drink this, amigo."

It was fine-tasting mescal. He nodded his approval after the first taste. Someone had a brought a pine casket. After Juanita had cleaned Jeminez's face and straightened his hair, they lifted him up and put him in the red-cloth-lined box. Men took the rope handles, and Slocum knew they were headed for the church. They wheeled away his slayer's body in a handcart.

When they drew near the small chapel, he could hear the sound of a pickax on gravelly ground as men began to prepare the final resting places for Jeminez and his killer in the cemetery next door. It was the first sign of haste he had ever seen among these people. Belle steadied the sobbing Juanita. Both were wearing shawls over their heads as they were guided to the front row of pews.

Slocum removed his hat and took a place at the rear. The assistant lighted candles and said prayers in Latin. The responses came from the audience in unison. A thick-bodied woman sang a hymn in Spanish. The bells tolled, and the assistant led the procession with Juanita and Belle behind him as the pallbearers brought the coffin. The others came after them. The sniffs and sobs of the women filled the night. Slocum was the last man outside, where candles in reflectors lined the way.

"Who will avenge his death?" a man asked under his breath, walking beside Slocum as their soles crushed the gravel in the street.

"It will be done."

"Good. He was a brave man."

Slocum nodded. "More than that even."

"*Sí.*"

When Don Jeminez's funeral was completed, the bush-whacker was dumped in his own space and no one stayed or listened as the assistant prayed over him.

"Señor, come," a woman said. "We are going to the Ortegas', where there is food for you and the señora."

"We don't want to be any—"

"You are no trouble. It is customary to have a meal. Come along." She took his arm and led him behind the widow and Belle to the well-lighted house.

There was plenty of spicy fresh food. The women at the Ortegas' must have prepared the food in the short time since Slocum and Belle had come back with the bodies. He sat cross-legged on the floor and spoke to those who came by.

At last he and Belle took Juanita home. He went on to the shed, leaving the two women alone to talk. Bone-tired, he undressed, dropped on the bed, and went to sleep. Later in the night, she awoke him by hugging her ripe form to him.

"How is Juanita?"

"Asleep. I don't know what she will do."

"Oh, she is a survivor."

Belle kissed the back of his neck. "I know the emptiness she feels. Go back to sleep."

He considered the MC outfit. Even driving their cattle halfway back to Texas would not settle it. His eyes closed, his thoughts drowned in sleep again.

13

Slocum rose when the rooster crowed. In the purple crack of dawn he stretched, pulled on his britches, and stepped outside to empty his bladder. He'd left Belle asleep. His eyelids, like the sunrise, began to open wide. In the blue cast on the land, he studied a half-grown shoat trotting by that no doubt had recently escaped a pigpen. Busy grunting to itself and bragging about its newfound freedom, the animal hurried down the wagon tracks in search of something to root up and eat.

Slocum laughed to himself as he put away his tool. Poor pig didn't realize how poor his reception would be when someone discovered him loose. Slocum stepped back inside as the spears of light shone through the open doorway and bathed Belle's naked form in gold.

"You up?" she mumbled.

"Yes," he said, sitting on a crate and pulling on his socks. He rather enjoyed his private view of her shapely figure.

She drew the flannel sheet over her and laughed. "What am I?"

"A nice artwork," he said, busy pulling on his boot.

"Oh, I'm now an artwork?"

"You'd make a good one."

She shook her head in disapproval. "Men are strange creatures."

"Ah, but what would women do without us?"

She held the sheet to her cleavage and laughed. "I don't want to know."

"Good," he said, and stomped his boots on the dirt floor. "We better eat and ride. They're bringing us the two fresh horses I arranged for last night. Señora Ortega is feeding us."

"I must go check on Juanita," Belle said, flying out of bed with a flash of her pear-shaped boobs and beginning to dress. "Juanita said she sent word to Campo last night and her sister would come and be with her."

"I'll go see about the horses."

"Should I meet you at the Ortegas'?" She was slipping her long legs in the canvas britches.

"That's fine. The horses should be ready." He took both saddles and left the rifles behind. "We can get them later."

"I'll bring them," she said. "Go ahead. I know you are anxious to get going."

"Thanks."

The two horses were out in front of the Ortega residence hitched at the rack, and two men rushed to take the saddles from him. One horse was a light red roan that was almost white. It was a tall alert-looking horse that he felt could carry him. The other was a bulldog-style bay horse, hardly twelve hands high, but plenty stout, and he figured fast as a cat in a short run. The blankets were placed on the horses by some men there, and the saddles cinched.

Slocum decided to try the roan once they had him saddled. The man who owned him swore he was broke, but had not been ridden in some time. With a grateful nod, Slocum checked the roan with the reins and swung in the saddle. He could tell the horse was upset, and checked him up close as he danced on eggs with his hooves. Scattering the onlookers, the roan went sideways for a while, and when Slocum urged him forward, he tried to duck his head. Slocum popped him good over the rump with the reins, and the roan sucked his tail up between his legs and cat-walked forward.

About that time, two dogs had discovered the errant shoat. They began to drive the trespasser down the narrow street, barking and snapping at him. The pig let out a high-pitched scream, racing straight toward the roan horse. It was as if it aimed to run right under the high-stepping roan, who must have thought the devil was coming to get him. Pig squealing, dogs growling and snapping, they came like a tornado of dust at the horse and rider.

The roan had all he could take. He stuck his head be-tween his front legs and went to bucking through the parked *carretas* and flying chickens and scared goats. Slocum was doing fine—sitting tall in his saddle—until he lost his right stirrup, and before the roan crashed into a coyote fence, he shucked him. He came close to landing on both feet, watching the roan pile up head-on into the stake fence. The roan ended up lying on his side and floundering to get up. Slocum ran over and slipped in the saddle satis-fied that, other than shaking the pony's dignity, the crash had not hurt him. At last on his feet, the roan soon felt the slap of leather reins and sidled back up the street much bet-ter mannered.

"Oh, Señor, oh, Señor," the owner said. "I am so sorry he bucked."

"He'll do me just fine."

Everyone there laughed.

After breakfast, Slocum and Belle left the ranch in a long lope. He wanted to catch the herd and be certain that Raul and his crew were getting along all right. Then, if they had time, he'd see about Booth and the MC bunch too. That could wait.

All signs showed Raul and his crew were making good

time moving the herd, and in late afternoon Slocum and Belle found the camp. The women were busy cooking and waiting for the men's return when they reached the cooking fires and camp setup. He left Belle with the camp crew and rode east.

Near sundown Slocum saw their dust. The men must have driven the steers back to Texas, he mused as he dismounted, pulled the crotch of his pants down, and shook his legs. The riders looked tired, but Raul smiled when they pulled up before him.

"Any problems?" Slocum asked.

"No, those cattle may still be running."

"Good. We lost Don Jeminez."

The frowns on the sunbaked faces of the dust-covered men registered their disappointment. They all began asking questions.

Slocum held up his hand. "A bushwhacker shot his mule out from under him. Either in the fall or something, he must have hit his head. He was dead when I found him. The back shooter is dead too."

"Good. We better get to camp. I am hungry," Raul said.

"I am sorry to hear about Don Jeminez's death," an older man said as he rode up to Slocum, who was mounting his roan.

"Yes, and they'll pay for it." He nodded to the gray-headed man and checked the roan.

The serious brown eyes met Slocum's. "Don Jeminez was a good man. I am not a pistolero, but I would ride with you when you take the war to them."

"*Gracias,*" Slocum said. "We will see."

The man nodded, and Slocum knew he meant what he had said. No telling how Slocum would handle that bunch, but the time was drawing near. With his eyes afire from the wind and dust, he set the roan in a long lope for camp with the dozen or so hands. In the west, the sun was fixing to settle beyond the horizon. Tired as he felt, he hoped he could sleep.

Belle shook him in the predawn. Then she snuggled her warm body against his as the cool air tried to enter their bedding. He blinked his gritty eyes and smiled at her while rolling on his side.

"Guess this is the day," he said.

"For what?"

"Find Booth and have this out. I figure the big man of the MC, whoever he is, is going to try one more hard play against the ranch. If he don't have Booth, he'll have someone worse." Wearily, Slocum exhaled and shook his head. "Don't matter. These folks will meet them with their teeth barred."

"Can they?"

"Never got too close to a leashed dog. He'll whip bears." Slocum kissed her and found the energy to get up—better yet, the willpower to leave her bare, sensuous body and to dress in the starlight Seated beside him, she put on her shirt and when she finished, gave him a shake with her hand on his shoulder.

"Better not do too much. You'll confuse me about what foot to put my boots on," he said.

She laughed and quickly pulled on her pants, standing above him on the bedroll. "I really don't mind this camping business, you know that."

"They all say that. Women all need a dry roof over their head, a good well, and an oven. That's three things this prairie don't offer."

"I'm talking about riding on with you—after—after—Harrigan."

He nodded. "I know, but my tracks get lots harder than this. No, someday we'll have to part, and I may not even get to kiss you good-bye, but you'll know."

"The Abbott brothers?" Her voice was a soft hush.

"Yes. They always get some leads."

"I'll try to remember that."

He rose and shook his pants legs down over his boot tops. "It won't be easy either."

She reached out, hugged and kissed him.

It was never easy to just up and leave a woman that special. He set out for their horses. Maybe by sundown he'd have this MC matter settled. After breakfast, and a long talk with Raul about his theory about the head man of the MC coming to the ranch with a show of his might, Slocum and Belle rode out.

The MC camp was probably eight to ten miles to the southwest. They short-loped and at mid-morning, they topped a rise and the two wagon tops could be seen in the bright sun. Slocum checked the loads in his pistol and reholstered it. Then he pulled down his hat and nodded to her.

"You stay back. There's liable to be trouble if Booth's there."

"I'm going in with you. I have a gun and can use it. Lead the way."

He shook his head at her in disapproval, but felt there was no way to argue her out of it. He raised the reins and sent the roan for the camp. A man in an apron came out and stared at the two riders. The sight of the cook told Slocum his man might not even be there.

"Don't get gun-happy, but when the cards are down, use it," Slocum said to her.

"I understand."

Slocum nodded and kicked the gelding into a lope. Short of the cook, he reined the horse up in a slide that peeled up dust, and Belle's bay did the same beside him.

"Where's Booth?" Slocum asked as the wind swept their dust away.

"Mister, you can see fur yourself he ain't here." The

man, with salt-and-pepper whiskers, spat tobacco to the side. "You the one?"

"One what?"

"One ran off all the help."

"I guess so. Why?"

The old man wiped his hands on the apron front as if in deep consideration, then looked up at Slocum. "Henry Martin'll nail your hide to the corral fur your troubles. I can tell you that fur sure."

"Well, you better load up or I'll be back and fire all this stuff. A gallon of kerosene will torch these wagons and then you can hotfoot it back to Texas."

"I ain't moving. You ain't my boss."

"I may not be your boss, but you've got ten minutes to get hitched and going. I'm not fooling with the likes of you any longer."

"Back of the wagon," Belle said to Slocum.

Slocum dropped off his horse using him for a shield. "Tell that sumbitch behind the wagon if he don't want that gun stuck up his backside, to toss it out and get where I can see him."

The .44 now in Slocum's fist, he cocked the hammer and the cook shouted, "Drop that damn gun or he'll kill both of us."

"Aw, shit—"

"You're going to think that," Slocum said, moving out from behind the horse with his six-gun ready.

A gun clattered on the ground and a disappointed-looking kid came out. Slocum saw no more sign of anyone else. "Get hitched up and out of here. I'm not wasting the whole day. Where's that other gunhand?" Slocum asked, searching around.

"You mean Kelsey or Burks?"

"Kelsey, I guess. Burks's dead."

"Damn—" The cook looked deflated. "Burks was a tough enforcer."

"He ain't now. Where's this Kelsey?"

Cook snorted. "That chicken-liver rode out a day ago. But the old man can find more. He won't take this easy."

"You better talk sense to that old man. These people own this land. Fenced or not, it's theirs and they ain't giving up a blade of it."

"Hmm, they don't know Henry Martin."

"Tell him there ain't any grass in that cemetery at the ranch. He better pick him a better place to die."

"You don't tell Henry Martin nothing, mister. I been with him since before the war."

"Then maybe he'll listen to you. Better tell him to have his pistol cocked when he comes to the ranch again."

"Oh, he will. Guess if them supply wagons had got here, he'd'a knowed about it already."

"They ain't coming."

The cook turned to the boy. "Get them damn mules hitched. We're starting back fur Texas."

The boy gave Slocum a wary look and headed out in a trot. He tripped over something, sprawled facedown on the ground, and picked himself up still stealing glances back.

"He needs a wet nurse," the cook said in disgust about his helper. "Your name's Slocum, huh?"

"Yeah. That's Belle."

He swept off his stained weatherbeaten hat and bowed to her. "Name's Jeremiah Kane. Why, you're about as pretty as anything I've seen since I left Austin, and that was ten years ago."

Slocum holstered his .44. "Don't forget to tell Martin what I said."

Kane narrowed his left eye at Slocum. "You ever told a bull buffalo anything?"

"No, but I've shot my share of 'em."

"I bet you have. I'll tell him that too." Kane shook his head and went off to load up. "Trust me, Slocum, you'll be hearing from him."

Slocum ignored his threat and nodded to Belle. "He's leaving."

Her lips tight, she looked things over one last time and said, "Yes." Then she turned her pony around. Stirrup to stirrup, they headed for the ranch.

At Juanita's house the next day, Slocum busied himself setting some new fence posts to keep her shoats in. Digging was slow, but he had one hole dug when he wiped his forehead on his sleeve. Soon, without a word, others joined him. The sound of iron crowbars chipping at gravel cemented in hard soil began to ring. Slocum nodded in approval. He sure thought he'd be a week making the new pen.

"When will they come?" Fernando asked quietly as the sounds of all the women at the house carried out to Slocum.

"I'm not certain. I sent the head man's cook home yesterday. He said the old man never took no for an answer."

"What is this old man's name?" someone else asked, busy tamping in the first post.

"Henry Martin."

They shook their heads. They'd never heard of him.

"He's a tough old codger, I figure, that aims to take what he wants and has in the past."

"You think he will come here?"

Slowly Slocum nodded. "That's why I'm fixing these pens. It is only a matter of time."

"What should we do?"

"We have two weeks—ten days, I figure, before he gets his new army ready. When the time gets closer, we'll set some dynamite charges out front. They want trouble, we'll give them what for."

"Will you be here?"

"If not, I'll give you the directions."

Satisfied, they went back to work. Days crawled by. They cleaned the irrigation ditches to Juanita's hay fields and garden. Mowed her alfalfa and stored it in the barn for her cow and two work mules. They fixed the roof on her casa, and brought her in a large supply of cooking wood all split and ready, plus a winter's supply of heating wood. Then they plastered two other houses that needed it.

Slocum spent his nights with Belle's silky body in his arms. They made deep love night after night. Each morning, with a hand on his sore back, he managed to get up and do another long day's work. The defenses were shored up. Firearms cleaned and oiled. Target practice became a part of each day.

The charges were set in a row at a range that would make a pistol shot useless, and three men knew where they were and when to light them. Two boys with field glasses kept guard each day a few miles out, and looked for the invaders or any telltale dust. For Slocum's part, he felt the time was growing near. But no one had come. Would the people give up on anyone coming? He hoped not.

"This ranch has never looked this nice," Raul said as the two lounged in chairs under Juanita's rethatched porch roof.

Slocum's legs were stretched out, and he slapped them and agreed. "That's why I stayed. I figure eventually he'll come. No way he's going to let some Messikins turn him away."

"I think we are ready."

"Yes, you are. He won't find people huddling in fear."

"Every day I look to the east and expect him to come."

"He will. It's in his mind that we whipped him and sent his cattle back."

"You don't know this man."

"No," Slocum said, reflecting on the matter. "But I know his kind and how they think."

14

The boy came riding in on his sweaty horse and jerked him to a stop. Pointing to the east and out of breath, he finally managed, "Much dust—many riders are coming."

"Good," Slocum said. It would finally come to a head.

"I will ring the church bell," one man said.

"No." Slocum caught him by the arm. "I don't want him to know that we know he's coming. Go to the fields and get everyone up here." He saw Raul running to join them. "Break out the rifles and ammo. They're coming."

"They're coming?"

"Yes," Slocum said. "Time to do what we've practiced. Everyone keep low so they don't see our preparations."

Belle came on the run. "I heard they are coming."

"The guard says so. It's been three weeks. He's had enough time to gather an army."

"What do I need to do?"

"I guess use a rifle. If you want to."

"I'm a better shot than most of the men."

He agreed and kissed her on the cheek. "Keep your head down. Use the loopholes we made in the wall."

"Yes, sir." Then she winked at him. "You do the same."

"I'll try." He went and saddled his horse, and led him

down to the wall in the event he needed him. The horse was tied with a rope rather than reins in case the shooting disturbed him. Slocum went back to scan the horizon.

"Manteca is back," Raul said about the other guard. "He counted over twenty men with rifles."

"He bring my glasses back?"

"Oh, *sí*." Raul took them from around his neck.

Slocum could see the boiling cloud of dust in the lenses. He hoped the invaders tried a frontal charge. That would mean he could concentrate his firepower on them. Martin would never suspect the battle he faced, but surprise was the best tool in war. Upsetting the enemy was worth a lot. All Slocum could do was hope it worked and that the farmer-herders all held tight and didn't lose their nerve.

Concealed behind the wall, men and their wives sat on the ground with weapons and ammo. Blankets were spread and *ollas* held drinking water. All the men needed to do was sit up and shoot out of the ports made in the thick wall. Then the women could reload their rifles while the men shot with other rifles or pistols.

Slocum had set up many boards for target practice at a range where he figured Martin and his men would open fire. The boards had been riddled with bullets. Everything had been long removed and the area swept clean. Now the defenders waited.

The sun reached high noon and he could see the riders in his glasses. A rider near the lead, with a snowy handlebar mustache, was pushing his sweaty gray horse hard, carrying a Winchester in his right hand. From the looks of the high-priced hat and the man's suit, Slocum figured that was Henry Martin.

Slocum wanted this bunch placed near the explosives set in the ground. He might have to ride out and stop them there. Raul and a man called Juan were telling everyone on the firing line to hold their fire until they gave the command. Otherwise there was silence, save for the hoofbeats drumming the ground in the distance.

A small boy ran out of a casa with his mother in hot pursuit. She swung him up and kissed him. But to no avail. He kept crying and shouting, "Daddy. Daddy, I want my daddy."

On his horse, Slocum rode to the gate. On the rise where he wanted them, the incoming riders began to fan out in a line, load their Winchesters, and look hard-eyed at the ranch.

"Henry Martin?" Slocum called out to the man holding up the rifle.

The rancher stretched his back and nodded. "You must be Slocum."

Slocum nodded. "I'm not packing a body back to Texas. You'll have an unmarked grave if you die up here today."

His words brought chuckles and scoffing words from the outfit.

"We'll take care of our own," Martin said. "Ain't no one running my outfit off the open range. You or no other damn greasers."

"This ain't Texas, Martin." The roan stomped the ground at a fly under him.

"I ain't figured how one damn busybody sent my crew packing. But you ain't sending this outfit packing—"

"Martin—" The riders drowned out Slocum's reply in angry shouts.

Slocum turned the roan and started back in the gate.

"Let's get 'em!" Martin screamed.

Behind Slocum, their rebel yells shattered the air. Inside the gateway, Slocum slipped off the roan and hit him on the butt. With the Winchester in his hands, he headed for the wall.

When he was two steps from the barrier, the explosives went off. A giant cloud of dust went up. He dove for cover beside Belle. Screams of horses and hurt men filled the air. Bullets from the ranch began to pour into the shadowy figures. Curses and cries of pain soon joined the ear-shattering shots pouring into them like an attack of hornets.

The sound of the men's voices from the ranch began to grow as the enemy wilted under their fierce gunfire. Soon, the wind swept the black powder smoke and dust away.

At last, the field was clear. Horses lay wounded and dead ones covered the ground. Human bodies were sprawled amongst them—some obviously dead, others moaning in pain.

Slocum held his hand up to cease the sporadic firing that still occurred. He could see the dust of some of the riders fleeing to the east. Those lucky enough to miss getting hit or blown up were escaping.

His crew stood up and shouted. Satisfied, Slocum nodded in agreement and headed for the field of dead and dying. When he reached the carnage, he dispatched a crippled horse with a pistol shot to the forehead. Behind the chestnut animal lay two motionless riders facedown who'd lost their hats. It was a grim, bloody scene.

"Get the dead ones out," he said, and the men obeyed.

"This one is still alive," Juan said, carrying the man by his arms, another man holding his legs. "What should we do with him?"

Slocum looked at the man whose fresh blood oozed from his dust-plastered face. "Set him by the wall for later."

They nodded and moved him there.

"Not one of our men were hurt," Raul said. "Will they come back?"

Slocum caught Raul by the sleeve, and they both looked down at the bleached pale face and snowy mustache of the man lying on his back between two dead horses. "Henry Martin won't."

On his knees beside the dead rancher, Slocum reached

over and closed the blue eyes that were staring unseeing at the clear sky.

"But we always must be ready?" Raul squatted across from him. "There will be others?"

"There will be others," Slocum said. "But after this day, they'll use more caution about the folks at the ranch."

Belle joined him later when the field was cleared. "What's the count?"

"Seven are dead. Five are wounded. Raul is having a wagon hitched to send them in to the doctor at Campo."

"How many got away?"

"Enough."

"Enough?"

"Enough to tell everyone in the West that the folks at this ranch are tough customers."

"What will we do?"

"Get us a packhorse outfit ready. Load up and head for Texas at first light. See if we can find Harrigan." He waited for her reply.

She gave him a grave nod. "Yes. I want him either on trial or dead for killing Hank. I never saw Booth among those riders. Did you?"

He shook his head. "No. I haven't figured that out either, unless the old man fired him over letting us run him and his cattle off."

"That cook wasn't with them either."

"He's probably out there making camp and waiting for them. He's been with the old man for years, he said."

"There's a fiesta tonight." She linked her arm in his.

"I better ride out and check out that camp. You got me thinking they might make another raid back here, thinking we'd not be looking for them. Get their revenge."

"What should be done?"

"I'll tell Raul to post guards till we're sure that they've turned tail and really run."

"Juanita has some food ready. Eat. You must eat something before you leave. Meet you there and I'll have our horses ready."

He started to say he would go by himself, then stopped. "Good. I'll tell Raul about the guards."

Slocum found the leader in his casa and told him to be ready in case they came back.

"*Sí*, we will post guards until you say it is safe. Will you be at the fiesta tonight?"

"No, I need to check on those left. We should be back tomorrow."

"I wish I could pay you. You have done so much for us."

Slocum shook his head. "I did this to honor Don Jeminez. He was my friend and I'll miss him."

"I savvy." Raul clapped him on the arm. "Still, you carried the banner well for your amigo."

"I hope they will continue to look after Juanita when we leave."

"I will see they do that. But they will."

Slocum shook his hand and hurried off, anxious to learn more about the remaining raiders. Where were they? And what were they planning to do?

He blinked at the sight of a rider leading a horse—Jeremiah Kane. Slocum strode out, waving Raul back as he went to meet the man.

Kane reined up his horse. "I told him you'd shot lots of old bull buffaloes. Guess he's dead?"

"He's dead."

"I reckoned he'd've liked to be buried in Texas." Kane spat aside and looked back at Slocum nodding at his decision.

"What about his army?"

With a snort, Kane shook his head. "That bunch of chicken-livered worthless cowards all ran off. They got to the wagon, loaded their things, and left. Said these Messikins had cannons and a Gatling gun."

Slocum laughed. "I can help you load him. His body's up by the church on the ground with the others."

"Ain't no need. I can find him. 'Preciate yeah letting me have him. It's what I owe him. A grave in Texas." Kane booted his horse on.

"Where's Booth?"

"Old man never mentioned him when he came out. Figured he fired him." Kane looked back, and then he shared a nod with Slocum before he went on. "Been just like him."

"What does he want?" Raul asked Slocum when he rode back in.

"The old man's body. Let him go. I think the war is over, but keep some guards out anyway. Oh, yes, I'll be here for the fiesta tonight. I better go tell Belle."

"Good," Raul said after him. "See you then."

Over lunch, he told Juanita and Belle about Kane coming for the body and his own impression that the war was over. They drank red wine to celebrate, and even Juanita acted more her old self.

"Siesta time," Belle announced when they finished eating. "And you need one. You were up for nights concerned about the defense of this place."

Slocum held up his hands to ward her off. "I am ready to take a nap."

She laughed, and moved over to hug his head with both arms wrapped around him. "I'm glad this is finally over."

"So am I." More than she'd ever imagine.

In the shed, at last alone, she began to undress him as he toed off his boots. Her furious fingers undid the shirt buttons and then tore open his pants, shoved his galluses down.

He had unbuttoned her shirt and held her breasts in the palms of his hands. Hefting them lightly, he grinned down at her. "Sweet, sweet."

"You're going to think sweet."

"I know I am." Her hand closed around his scrotum and

made him stand on his toes. Her actions silenced him and he kissed her. She soon began stroking his hardening dick.

"Oh, gawd, I need you," she huffed.

"Yes," he agreed as she shed her britches and lowered herself on the bed. Then she crawfished on her back to the head of the bed to get in place. Her firm breasts were heaving and swinging, and his stomach sank at the vision of her figure in motion. He gazed for a long moment at the breathtaking sight of her nakedness. His butt ached to stab her clear through as he put a knee on the bed and the ropes creaked.

Then he moved between her open legs to enter her tight gates. It took his breath away when the swollen head of his dick met her ring. With gentle pressure, his sensitive erection slipped past it and she sighed. Then she smiled, raising her butt off the bed for his deeper entry as he pumped in and out.

The world tilted and their fierce efforts required all the air they could huff in. His pounding grew faster and harder. The ropes under the mattress creaked in protest as he sought the contracting inside her. His erection tingled with electricity with each plunge. His brain swirled in a maelstorm—relief—relief. Then, from the depth of his scrotum came the cramping that made his spine jerk upright and slam the skintight head hard against her wall. He exploded. All his energy went out with the ejaculation that flooded her and they collapsed in a pile. Done in.

15

A rooster awoke him. The shrill crowing shattered the cool morning air. It was still dark outside, and he slipped on his pants and went to the doorway to study the high cloud formation on the horizon shielding the sunup. Gingerly, on his bare feet, he moved aside to find a place to pee in the pickly pear plant beside the barn. The stream splashed off the adobe wall until at last his bladder was empty. He turned, listening to the meadowlarks and doves. Somewhere a milk cow was bawling for her calf.

On tender feet he made his way back to the doorway, and soon sat on the edge of the bed. He brushed off the bottoms of his feet and put on his socks. Then he pulled on each boot before he turned to Belle's still-sleeping form.

"We better head for Texas in the morning."

In a sleep-tinged voice, she finally managed, "I guess so."

"I'll fix the shoes on our horses today. And get us some food to take along."

"I'm going to get dressed," she said, sweeping her hair back. Scooting on her butt to the edge of the bed in her snowy nakedness, she laughed. "I'm going to really miss this bed."

"The hard ground won't be the same." He tucked in his shirt, put up his galluses, and then strapped on his holster.

"Better get a bath today. We may be some time in the saddle before we get another."

"You're right. How far are we away from where Harrigan's supposed to be?"

"A week to ten days by my calculations. But he may be off collecting bounties for all I know."

She paused in pulling on her pants. "I never thought about that."

"The country we're going to cross is tough too. It's the country the Comanche used to call home. There isn't much law out there or water either."

Nodding that she understood, she rose and pulled up her britches. "I can make it."

"I know that. I just wanted to warn you."

"At times I wonder why you're helping me."

He stepped over, put her face between his palms, and kissed her. When he removed his lips, he smiled at her. "That reason enough?"

"I guess so." Then she wrinkled her nose. "Poor pay."

They both laughed and hurried off to the house for Juanita's breakfast.

The day passed fast. A few shoes were reset and the ponies were ready. Slocum bought some good jerky from one lady that Juanita recommended. A fifty-pound sack of frijoles from another. Ground corn and brown sugar mix from a third person. And Juanita found some raisins and dried apples to pack in their panniers.

"I will miss Belle," Juanita said to Slocum when they were alone for a moment. "I wish she would stay. I fear for her chasing down murderers. That is work for a man. I know she is a very strong-willed woman. Very determined, but I worry for her going on."

"You could not talk her out of it."

"No, I have tried."

Slocum nodded and strapped the pannier shut. "I leave

you with a heavy heart about your loss. If there was any way I could have saved him—"

She rushed over and hugged Slocum. "He knew his business. He saved the ranch. He did not die in vain."

"Still—"

"She pressed a finger to his mouth to silence his protest, stood on her toes, and kissed him. "God be with you. Come by and see me when you pass this way again. My door will always be open."

"I will, Juanita. I will."

They left before the rooster crowed the next morning. Juanita had packed in their saddlebags food for that day. On a lead, the packhorse carried their cooking gear, food supplies, and bedding. They rode southeastward into another shield of clouds that obscured the sunrise that morning.

At mid-afternoon, pushing hard, they ran into some light showers. They moved on, and an occasional touch of moisture swept over them on the gusts of wind.

Late in the day, a Texas flag on a mast attracted their attention. It was flying over a few adobe hovels, and Slocum and Belle rode cautiously toward them.

"These places are tough," he said, looking over their back trail and, satisfied, turning back. "Usually they are frequented by men on the dodge. Probably was an Indian trading post at one time."

She nodded. "What are your plans?"

"Water the horses and move on. I wouldn't sleep within ten miles of here."

"You've been here before?"

He shook his head as they rode stirrup to stirrup. "No, but I've been in the same sort of outpost. They're up and down west Texas and New Mexico."

"I'll keep my pistol ready."

"Don't hesitate to use it."

"Oh, I won't."

"There's a water tank. Water the horses and I'll go inside and check on things."

"I can handle that easy." She gave him a big smile.

He nodded, satisfied that she could do just that. The place niggled at him. Alone, he'd not have thought twice about stopping, ordering some rattlesnake-head whiskey, and going on. At the empty hitch rack he dismounted, gave Belle the reins, looked around, and saw only a young boy leading a protesting small goat. Slocum moved aside the moth-eaten buffalo robe that served as a door, and entered the cavelike interior lighted with smoky candles.

"Howdy, mister," a rusty-voiced man said. He stood behind the bar wearing a top hat, white shirt, and black silk vest.

Not satisfied with the room's emptiness, Slocum eyed the dust-coated tables, then walked to the bar. It had been a rather fancy setup at one time, but scars and notching had marred its appearance. "What do you call this place?"

"Free Water. I'm Gibbs, owner, bartender, trader, and mayor."

Slocum nodded. "Guess you've got whiskey."

"By the shot or by the bottle?"

"Double shot'll be fine."

Gibbs produced a glass and poured the brown liquor in it. "Four bits."

Slocum slapped the money on the bar. "You the only one around?"

He pocketed the coins in his vest. "Yeah, me, my wives, and my children right now."

Slocum raised the glass to him. "Here's to your health and all your extended family."

"By the way, are you hungry?"

"We've got food. My partner's watering the horses. We'll be moving on."

The man nodded his head. "We can cook you a fine fat goat. Only cost fifty cents for the two of you."

"Thanks, we'll be moseying on."

"Getting late in the day. You and your friend could spend the night here."

"Thanks," Slocum said, and downed the last of the whiskey. "Maybe next time."

"Come again," Gibbs said, and wiped his hands on a bar rag.

"Next time I'm through here," Slocum said, and pushed the heavy hide aside to go outside.

He joined Belle at the tank.

"What do you think?"

"I think he lies. See those three ponies in the corral?" He indicated some mustangs with dried salt on their backs where saddles had once sat. They'd been rode hard and put up wet—recently too.

She nodded. "They were rode in here, right?"

"Yes. I wonder where the riders are at. He claims there's only his wives and kids here."

"Wives?"

With a grin for her, he nodded. "Probably Indian women or breeds. They aren't too valuable in trade out here."

She shook her head in dismay. "Are we riding on?"

"Yes." Definitely. He wouldn't sleep except with one eye open at this outpost, even alone.

They mounted up and rode away. Slocum could feel some cold eyes staring at his back. No need to turn and look. They were hidden, but they'd watched Slocum's and Belle's every move since they'd arrived there. The thing that bothered him the most was having her along. He could handle himself—always had thus far. But her being there made a big difference in how he did things.

He nodded for Belle to move out, and they short-loped for the next horizon. In an hour it would be sundown. The more space they had between them and Free Water, the better he'd feel.

Twice he'd paused and used his field glasses on their back trail for any sign of trail dust. Nothing. That did not make him feel any easier. They were ripe meat for the two-legged buzzards that existed in this no-man's-land.

A half hour later, they found some cottonwoods around a seep. Several wild horses had recently been there. The water was in the tracks and their own horses, not too thirsty, only tasted it. He hobbled and unsaddled them while Belle started a fire with the dead branches on the ground. The bloody sunset was swallowed by the thick cloud banks and he knew there would be no twilight. In fact, he'd heard some distant thunder rumbling. It might really rain.

She made coffee, and they had some tortilla-wrapped bean burritos to eat that Juanita had sent along.

"You've been awfully quiet all day," she said, seated cross-legged close by him. The shifting wind sent the low fire's smoke in their eyes, then away again.

"Been concerned about trouble. There's been hundreds of people never seen again that wandered out here."

"I thought that was because of the Indians."

He took the hot tin cup in both hands, shook his head, and blew on the steam. "No, there were about as many worthless white renegades out here as there were Indians. Some you couldn't tell that they were white."

"In other words, they lived off those folks headed west."

"They never raided a big wagon train. Except maybe to steal some stock or some supplies. But they swarmed on the small outfits and people traveling alone. Then they burned the wagons so Indians got all the blame."

"Why didn't the law do something?"

"Vast country and not many lawmen."

"I understand that. More coffee?" She rose and turned her head to listen. "That thunder sounds closer."

He tossed some twigs in the red-hot fire and they were

consumed. "I'll string the tarp tree to tree and we'll have some shelter."

"Oh, I'll be fine."

He wanted to say, *Until we finally arrive—yes—you'll be fine till then.* But he nodded instead and went to string the rope to cover the panniers and themselves so they'd be dry in case the storm blew in.

When the the rope was tied off, he made their beds between the panniers, then he draped the canvas over the tree-to-tree rope waist-high to form a low tent over them. She joined him and drove in more stakes for tie-downs as the wind increased and the sky wall in the west became illuminated with vivid bolts of lightning.

Soon the first beads of hail swept in on a cold wind. He had all their gear under the shelter and crawled in to join her—grateful he'd finished in time, he hugged and kissed her. In the background, the fire sizzled out. The stink of wet ashes swirled inside their shetter as the rain grew stronger.

"Think they'll be out in this weather?" she asked in the darkness snuggled in his arms.

"Wolves never really den up. They keep pacing back and forth waiting for the right moment."

"When will be the right moment for them?"

"When you'd least expect them or when they figure you'd given up and gone to sleep."

Soon larger hail began to beat on their canvas roof. The fire went out. They sat in the shelter looking out the small eastern opening. Every few seconds, the night was illuminated by the lightning, the ground trembling under them from the blasts. The storm tore at their shelter. Then he heard the horses whinny.

"Damn," he swore under his breath. "They're stealing the horses."

"What can we do?"

He drew his six-gun and started out. "You stay here. Keep your gun handy."

She nodded in the dim light of the flash outside. "Be careful."

He rushed out into the cold rain. With the next bolt that lit up the grove of trees, he saw a rider coming hard shooting at the tent, the orange flashes of his revolver blazing away, the bullets striking the canvas cover in the deluge of hard rain.

Slocum snapped off two shots at him, and the riderless horse shied from the man and raced off in the night. Where were the others? He could hear the protesting sounds of their own horses being driven away. He was too late. They were gone.

He found the rider on the ground facedown. Rivers were running down his own face and blinding him in the inky darkness. He picked up the rifle and decided the man was either dead or would be. The rest were gone. It would be daylight before he found anything more.

"Belle?" he asked, ducking down on his knees to enter the tent.

No answer.

He tossed the rifle inside and scrambled to where he found her on her back—not moving. Hands trembling, he dug out a dry match and lighted it. A knot formed in his stomach at the sight of her. The brief span of light showed her blank eyes staring at the ceiling. No. No.

16

He dug her grave with a rifle butt. It took hours. But at last he had a hole deep enough. Numb to the core with grief, he lifted her canvas-wrapped body and lowered it in to the grave.

Then, on his knees, he prayed. "Lord, take her home. She was dealt a tough hand out here by some of the devil's men. Belle belongs up there. I'll send *them* home too. Amen."

He rose and began to cover her up. When he finished, he'd still not seen a horse since the night before. Even the dead outlaw he'd left for the buzzards—his horse had run off. So Slocum wrapped his field glasses, saddlebags, canteen, and a small bedroll in his slicker with some jerky and a rifle. The rest he cached under the tarp. Then he picked up his slicker and started out for Free Water.

No need for a map, or even checking on the hoofprints in the muddy spots—he knew where he was going. It was never easy to forget a good woman. All day he hiked, keeping under the brow of any ridge until evening. Then he sat cross-legged on the high ground and studied the bloody sundown. It was the first time he'd eaten anything that day.

The hard smoky-tasting jerky was no treat. Nothing had lifted his spirits all day. All day he'd walked, one boot ahead of the other as if each footfall was stomping on her killers. Only they were not stomping hard enough to suit him. With no idea how much farther it was to Free Water, he rose in the night, gathered his things, and pushed on under the thousands of stars.

In the moonlight, at last he could see the flag flapping in the night wind. He found secluded place and waited. After dozing a few hours, he was jerked awake by the sounds of goats bleating. In the dim light of predawn, he could see some figures milking them. They looked like Indian women at the distance. No sign of the men—the killers. They were no doubt sleeping.

The goats were herded back in pens until sunup. The women, and the children helping them, went inside. He took a rifle and left the rest of his gear on the rise. In a low run he headed for the jacales. Catching his breath with his back to an adobe wall, he checked the rifle's chamber—loaded. Then he edged to the rear deciding to try the first jacal on the left. At the open door he could hear someone snoring. He slipped inside and found a man sleeping away on a pallet.

He set the rifle down. On his knees, he stuck his six-gun in the man's face. "One wrong move you're dead."

"Huh?" The man blinked his eyes in disbelief.

"Get on your belly. Hands behind your back."

"*Sí, sí.*"

Slocum found a reata, and tied his hands. "Where are the others?"

"Who?"

With his skinning knife in his hand, he applied the keen blade to the man's throat "Who is here?"

"Ah, Armando, Chico—Gibbs—some squaws."

"Where's Armando?"

"Huh?"

"What jacal is he in?"

The man shook his head. "He don't sleep inside. He's a breed."

"Chico?"

"I think he slept with one of the women."

"Which one?"

"Twila."

"Where's her place?"

"It's the one on the far side of the saloon."

"You make a sound you're dead." He sheathed his knife and rose. Rifle in his hand, he checked outside before stepping out in the growing light. Then he hurried around the saloon and studied the jacal from the corner of the building.

Voices of women carried from the rear of the saloon. Cooking-fire smoke entered his nostrils and the food smelled good. It was fifty feet to the doorway of the jacal. He rushed to it and stepped inside. He felt the dark eyes on him. Eyes of a cornered weasel as the man raised up on his elbow. Then the man moved like one—started to twist for the six-gun on the floor.

Slocum's finger closed on the trigger and the rifle spat lead in an ear-shattering blast. His hand slipped down in the lever and ejected the cartridge. Then he shot again into the body, which was in the thrashing throes of death. Bullet number two slapped him like the thud of an impact on a watermelon. Number three smashed his forehead.

Rifle reloaded, he whirled and started out the door. Gibbs came around the corner, dressed in his underwear and brandishing a Walker Colt. Slocum dropped to his knees and fired at his chest. The man's Colt muzzle spat a bullet into the dust. Gibbs's knees buckled and, struck hard by the second rifle shot, he fell over backward.

Slocum could hear the horses, and rushed around to the front of the saloon. Two riders were racing away, bareback on horses from the corral. His chances of hitting either were small, so he eased the trigger down. His prisoner was one of the men, the other must have been Armando.

"Oh!" wailed a distraught woman coming from behind the buffalo hide.

"Who were those two?" he demanded.

She looked at him terrified and shook her head as if she didn't know.

"Who were they?"

"Armando and Felipe."

"Where do they live?"

She turned up her light-colored palms and shook her head. "Where do such *bandidos* live?"

"Gibbs was in it with them."

"I don't know."

He reached out and shook her shoulder with one hand. "You know. You know damned good and well. He sent them to steal my horses and murder me."

"Please, Señor, I know nothing." She began to cry and cowered away from him.

"I'll hang you, woman, if you don't tell me the truth."

"Yes, yes, he did."

"Those three worked for him?"

"Yes, yes, they did."

"They killed the lady rode in here with me a day ago."

She dropped her chin. "I'm sorry."

"They will be too. Now I need some food."

"There is food." With a twist of her head she indicated inside the saloon.

"I know, I can smell it" He motioned for her to go first, and he ducked inside the hide doorway after her.

The three women served him frijoles, corn tortillas, barbequed goat, and white cheese melted over enchiladas. They were all young Indian women. Ula was the one that Slocum had talked to. She was part Mexican and had sharp facial features. Tina was more Indian with slanted eyes and high cheekbones—tall for her race and thin, in her late teens. The very pregnant girl, and youngest, they called Ono. He thought her to be maybe fourteen. All had ended up there as slaves.

"What can we do now? He is dead." Tina stood with her arms folded over her chest and backed by the other two.

"Arm yourselves. Be tough and make this your home." They had no place else to go. "Can any of you count money?"

"Ono can, she went to Indian school," Tina indicated.

"Make her the keeper of it. Be tough traders when the whiskey men come by. Keep your guns loaded. You either kill them or they kill you."

"What will you do?" she asked.

"Go after them. They killed the lady who rode with me." Finished and unable to eat any more, he pushed the plate away.

"You could stay here. Run this place." She used her long fingers to indicate the interior of the saloon.

He shook his head. "I'm leaving two horses here. There is some gear south of here at the camp where they shot her. Go get it and if I don't return in six weeks, you may have it too."

Tina nodded.

He put some money down and she shook her head.

"No, everyone must pay," he said. "You savvy?"

"Everyone must pay," she repeated as if she had to learn it.

"Everyone."

He went out and saddled his roan with a worn-out saddle from the corral's top rail. They'd taken Belle's bulldog mountain horse. Good, he'd be easy to identify. He hugged each of the women, mounted up, and rode to the rise for his things. He tied them on the saddle, then headed east with a glance back at Free Water. They might make it.

Late in the day, he stopped at a low-walled ranch house with a creaking windmill that needed greasing badly. A tall woman in her twenties came out holding a rifle on her hip.

She had a willowy figure. The wind swept the blue calico dress around her legs, but her clear blue eyes were devoid of anything but serious business.

"Evening, ma'am," he said, removing his hat.

"You can water your horse, mister. Then ride on."

"Thank you. Did two men riding bareback come through here today?"

"You mean that worthless Messikin and breed?"

"Could be."

"Those two and some others stole three horses from us not a month ago."

"Three of them are dead."

"They worked for that buffoon Gibbs at Free Water, didn't they?"

"Yes, ma'am. He's dead."

She blinked hard at him. "Sounds like you've sure been cleaning up this country."

"Three nights ago they raided our camp. They shot a good friend of mine."

"Well, those two rode through here about three hours ago. I kept my rifle on them the whole time. Better put that horse in the pen when you get him watered. There's hay in there. I've got some chili on the stove."

"I'm obliged," he said, and touched his hat brim before he dismounted.

"Anyone shot Gibbs needs some reward." She started to turn on her heel. "I'll put a wash pan out and a towel for you."

"Yes, ma'am." He watched her go back inside and guessed her to be in her early twenties. Sharp-edged as the west Texas wind, she was tough enough to survive. He wondered about her man and family. This looked like an operating cow ranch. He'd been so intent on tracking those two, he hadn't bothered to notice the brand on the cows and calves in the mesquite and bunchgrass.

He led the pony to the tank and let him drink while he

undid the latigos. There were two good ponies in the pen. They were freshly shod using horses that showed from the white saddle scars on their withers that they were working cow ponies.

With his horse in with the rest, he took off his hat and combed his fingers through his hair. He felt unfit to enter the woman's house. Bathless and smelling more horse than human, he considered himself hardly fit for a campfire gathering, let alone to go inside the house of a white woman. At the porch he hung his hat on a peg, rolled up his sleeves, and used the yellow bar of lye soap on his hands in the warm water in her enameled pan that had been set out on the gray weathered table.

He washed his face with palms of water, and realized his beard was grown out. Then, using the towel, he dried his face and looked off at the west. A softer sunset was sinking out there than the night before. When he turned, the woman was on the porch.

"Ready to eat?"

"I sure am. Your husband's not here?"

"Tascosa. Getting supplies, won't be home for days. If he comes back then."

"Oh."

"Frank drinks a lot. He'll eventually come home. Bring a few hands with him for me to feed, and they'll be around till roundup in the fall. Then they'll go back to Tascosa and he'll come back alone whenever he thinks about it."

"Just leaves you out here alone?"

She turned back and laughed. "That's what a woman is for, right? Take care of things while he dances with some hussies in the Bye Gilly Saloon."

When he didn't reply, she pulled out the chair for him at the table. "I'm a dutiful wife."

"I never doubted that."

"Well, now you know my situation. Have a seat and eat before it gets cold."

"Thanks." He studied the rich-looking chili in the large crock and the soda crackers beside it as he sat down. "You aren't eating?"

She poured him coffee. "In Frank Waters' house, men eat first. I am well trained."

"Since he ain't here and ain't going to be, get you a bowl. I like good company to go with good food."

A pleased look swept her face and some of the sternness dissolved in her facial expression. She nodded in approval. "I'll just do that."

"Where do you hail from?"

"Missouri." She had her back to him as she dipped out some chili from the kettle on the range. "We left there after we got married and wandered around until he gathered enough cows to stock this ranch. This place had been homesteaded and the man died, so his wife sold out to us. Frank's twelve years older than I am."

"So the windmill and all were here then?"

"Oh, yes, all the improvements were here. All we had to do was move in. Up till then I'd spent most of my married life in a covered wagon."

Between bites, he pointed his spoon at her across the small table. "I bet that was a treat to a woman."

"I wasn't certain that I could even live in a house."

They both laughed. Then she dipped her face down, looking a little embarrassed.

"I say something wrong?" he asked.

She shook her head. "I haven't laughed in years. Guess I felt silly doing it Frank would say so. Laughing's for fools."

"He must be a bundle of joy to live around." Slocum dipped a cracker in the red chili and chewed on it, looking hard at her.

"I told you, I am a dutiful wife."

"Well, duty be damned. You sure must be in a pickle of a deal."

Her steel-blue eyes met his. "I am. Miles from any-where or anybody. I can't go home, so I endure Frank Waters, this ranch, and the isolation. Last woman I talked to came passing by here with her family in a wagon seven months ago."

"What can I do about it?"

"Do you dance?"

"Yes. I don't suppose he dances either?"

"No. He considers it kid stuff. I have a music box—" She scooted her chair back. "I will play it."

"Sure."

She whirled and frowned at him. "I am not being too imposing on you, am I?"

"No, but I thought coming in here I smelled more like a horse than a man."

She laughed, and then put her hands to her face. "And I don't even know your name."

"Slocum."

"Very well, Mr.—"

He waved her words away. "Slocum, that's all." Wiping his face on the napkin beside the bowl, he rose and watched the swirl of her dress as she crossed the room to the music box. She raised the lid and used the key to wind it.

He stopped a few feet behind her. When she turned and the music began, his right hand slipped behind the small of her back and the other closed on her long fingers. They spun around the gritty floor to the waltz music, and soon she began laughing. He clutched her closer and felt her hip bone against his upper leg. She was thin, but she could dance and her hilarity proved contagious. Soon they both were laughing with an excitement that clutched at them as they danced. Then the music slowed and she rested her face against his shoulder. They were alone on another star— another place.

He raised her chin and kissed her. A kiss that sparked a fire in the tinder of all her suppression. Her hands clutched his head and her tongue sought his mouth—eager, excited, and demanding. His hands cupped her hard butt so she was tight against him.

At last she tore her mouth away and looked out of half-closed eyes at him. "I want you to take me."

He swept her up in his arms and she giggled. "Am I really doing this?" she said.

"I think so."

She put a hand to her forehead. "I've at last gone crazy, haven't I?"

"No, but it can get worse." He set her down on her feet at the edge of the bed and toed off a boot.

Caught up in her laughter, she put a hand on his shoulder to catch herself. "I sure don't have what you'd call a ripe form."

"You warning me?"

She stopped unbuttoning the dress and stopped laughing. "I mean it. Franks says—"

His finger on her lips silenced her. "I don't give a damn what Frank says."

She hunched her shoulders and shook her head in amused amazement. "You don't, do you?"

"No, ma'am."

"Francie—he calls me Frances, but with all my friends I grew up around it was Francie."

"Francie it shall be." He damn sure wasn't calling her any name her husband used.

"Well—" She looked back at the bed, then at him. The dress was unbuttoned and the small breasts were half-exposed.

"Want me to blow out the candle?" he asked.

"No, I want to remember this for a long, long time."

"All right." He slipped the dress off her and put it on the chair with his gun belt and his shirt. Then, with their gazes locked on each other, he shed his pants.

When she glanced down at his half-full erection, immediately her look went to the ceiling and she hugged him. "Good gosh, I didn't know men came in that size."

"Afraid?"

Laughing so hard her apple-sized breasts shook, she covered her mouth with her hand and swallowed. "No, I can't wait."

With the covers pulled back, she dropped on the bed and swung her slender white legs up. He slipped between them and lowered himself on top of her. Eyes tightly closed, she reached down blindly for his shaft, and sighed when she started it in to her gates. Then, laughing, she raised up for him to go deep inside her.

"Oh, my Gawd!" she cried out loud.

The bed protested under them. Their wild surging soon greased their bellies with perspiration and she was shouting, "I love it—love it—love it."

Their pubic bones mashed tight, her walls began to contract and her clit started to scratch the top of his turgid rod as he sought more and more of her. Their world swirled around them in wild abandonment. Breathing became huffing and their all-out effort grew to a peak, and then when he felt the time was at hand, his spine jerked him upright and he came hard.

She fainted.

"Oh, my Gawd—" she moaned, then blinked at him. "What's wrong?"

"Company. Outside," he whispered, and slipped off the bed to cross over and blow out the two candles on the table.

"Who?"

"I'm not sure, but I heard horses."

17

"Hey, woman, open up. We want some pussy." Someone drunk was pounding at the door.

In the dim starlight invading the room, she shook her face, hurrying to dress.

"Open up—you gawdamn whore! We come to fuck you." The drunk punctuated his speech with heavy blows on the solid door. "You better open up or I'll kick the damn door down."

"You open the door. I'll jerk him inside," Slocum said in her ear. "Then slam it shut."

She nodded, and they worked their way across the dark room to the entrance.

"Open up—"

"All right," she said to the intruder and raised the bar. "I'm hurrying."

When she swept the door open, Slocum caught the man by the shirt, jerked him inside, and bashed him over the head with his pistol butt. He collapsed on the floor with a grunt. Slocum used his knee to press him down and took his gun and knife from him.

"Got some cord?"

"Yes." She ran for it.

Slocum tied the intruder's hands and left him facedown. Then he began to dress.

"Which one is he?"

"Felipe is what they call him. The real tough one is the breed out there. Oh, I'm so grateful you are here."

"Damn you, Felipe, where did you go?" a voice outside called. "Where in the hell are you?"

Slocum could hear him riding back and forth in front of the door on his horse. Six-gun in his fist, Slocum nodded for her to open the door again. She raised the bar as quietly as she could and then pulled it open.

"Damn you—"

Slocum's Colt fired at the outline of a man balancing a rifle. He fell off the far side of his horse, and was on his feet like a cat running for the corral and outbuildings. The horse blocked Slocum's shot, and he moved past the frightened animal to look for the outlaw. Armando was gone from sight. Down there—somewhere—were the corral and outbuildings. And there was no sign in the starlight of Armando's rifle on the ground—wounded or not, he'd be like a diamondback rattler.

Slocum stepped back into the house. "That other outlaw awake?"

"He's moaning."

"Good, I'm using him for a shield. The other one is down by the corral and windmill."

"Be careful, they're dangerous." She put a hand on his arm. "But I've never had any dealings with the likes of them."

"I know that."

"Good. I've never denied anyone a drink here. But I sure never encouraged them to stay a minute longer."

"Francie, I know you didn't."

In the shadowy light, a smile crossed her face. "I like you to call me that."

He jerked Felipe to his feet. The half-groggy outlaw, smelling of rotgut, stood unsteadily. "Who are you?"

"Slocum's my name. You killed a friend of mine."

"That good-looking woman, huh?"

"Yes, now we're going to the corral. You better holler loud for Armando to give up and not shoot you."

"He won't give up."

"You better talk him into it." Slocum shoved him out the door and drew his Colt. He caught the man by the shoulder and told him to stop. Taking time to reload all six cylinders, he cocked the pistol and then motioned for him to move ahead.

"Armando! Armando! Don't shoot, it is me, Felipe. Please don't shoot, *mi amigo.*"

"If you fall down or try anything. I'll shoot you," Slocum warned. "Keep more right." Then, with a shove in the back with his muzzle, he sent his shield where he wanted him to go.

The outlaw kept up his pleading. Slocum studied every shadowy place for any sign of the other one. Then, from the side of the saddle shed, a rifle shot blazed in orange and the hot lead thudded into Felipe like something hitting a ripe watermelon.

Slocum answered with rapid fire from his pistol, and he knew when his second bullet struck something besides adobe wall. He advanced, his arm out, the Colt cocked and ready. Moving up to the slumped figure on the ground, he kicked the rifle away and bent over to feel for any sign of life. No pulse.

"Slocum? Slocum, are you all right?" Francie called, sounding uncertain as she walked toward him.

"It's over." He reached out and hugged her shoulder. Resting his cheek on top of her head, he rocked her with his free arm. "It's over."

Finally, he let go of her and spun the cylinder to an empty cylinder, then holstered the gun. "It's all over, Francie." His arm over her shoulder, he herded her toward the house.

"He even gunned down his own partner." She glanced at the silent Felipe on the ground and shook her head in disapproval as they went by him.

"There isn't any loyalty among them," Slocum said.

"They shot a woman?"

"Yes. I was helping her find her husband's killer. We got mixed up in a New Mexico range war on the way down here. You ever hear of Henry Martin and the MC?"

"He's a friend of Frank's."

"Well, not anymore. He's dead. He was all set to take over some rangeland in New Mexico and sent in lots of gunhands with his foreman and lost."

"I'm not surprised—last time that he was here, he bragged that he was moving there and that all he had to do was shoot a few greasers."

"He did, and in the end they shot him instead. He cost me a good friend that they dry-gulched."

"Who was the woman?"

"Belle Nelson. Some bounty men in Wyoming gunned down her unarmed husband thinking he was some outlaw. She took out a couple of them. We were headed south looking for the sole survivor."

"Guess you help lots of folks." She paused at the doorway.

"I do what I can. Where can I find Booth, the MC foreman?"

"He kill your friend?"

"Either did it or ordered it done."

"Tascosa. Probably drinking with Frank and hugging some hussy."

He nodded, and washed his hands in the cool water left in the basin.

"I can get you some fresh water," she said.

"Don't need it. Still a couple of hours till daylight. They can wait for their funeral." He finished drying his hands and pulled her to him. His mouth closed on hers and her hands soon clutched his head. Still a couple of hours left to tear up a bed with her.

He looked back at the starlit yard to check on things. She quickly pulled him inside and shut the door.

Following the brief burial of the two outlaws behind the sheds, he had greased the windmill. It did a lot less creaking and complaining when the wind came up that afternoon. He had shaved and bathed, and his clothes were drying on the line as he sat in Frank's loose-fitting pants and shirt on the porch bench, sipping on her fresh coffee. He felt halfway human.

"What next?" she asked, snuggled up close to him with her legs tucked under her dress.

"I need to go and find Booth."

"Will it do much good?"

"Every time you eliminate one rattler, they can't hatch any new ones."

"Why couldn't you have come along and married me instead of Frank?"

" 'Cause I was on the run and couldn't have stayed."

She frowned and flipped back her hair before laying her head on his shoulder. "You're still on the run?"

"Yes."

"Why aren't you in Mexico then?"

He blew on the hot coffee. " 'Cause I like it better up here. I'm not a Mexican. I'm a gringo down there regardless of how well I speak their lingo."

"So you will ride off and leave me?"

"I have to. Besides, Frank's coming back, you said."

"He always does whenever he gets damn good and ready.

"Slocum, I'd take living in a hut, or in a wagon even, over this life with him. I can ride a horse, shoot fair. Take me with you."

"Francie, if it was only me, I would. But I don't know when I'll have to disappear."

She shook her head on his shoulder. "Damn, if you ever ride by here and don't stop and see me, I'll—oh, well, be mad. I don't care if Frank's home or not."

"I'll remember that."

"Fat chance you'll ever get this far out of your way, isn't it?"

"Oh, you never know."

She wrapped her arm around his waist. "It's like having a real honeymoon, having you."

"Good, let's honeymoon. I can fix the fence in the morning."

"You don't have to fix that. I can do it after you leave."

"You running me off?"

"Lord, no." She was on her feet pulling him by one arm toward the open door. "Let's honeymoon."

18

A week later he headed for Tascosa. It was sure hard to part with her. Those things were never easy. He left with plenty of food in a cloth poke to eat on the way and the smell of her sweet musk embedded in his nostrils. She rode a few miles with him and they parted at mid-morning. He leaned over, kissed her, and then reined his pony away from her dun.

"See yah," he said, and she bit her lip unable to speak. She could only nod at him with wet lashes.

"I won't forget you and where you are, Francie."

He looked back from the next rise and waved to her. Still sitting her horse in place, she waved back. Then he was gone.

He camped out the next two nights, and the third day he found Tascosa. At the livery he stabled his horse for two bits a day, and started down the boardwalk. Before he left the wagon yard, the hustler pointed out Waters's team and saddle horse in the pen. Slocum tipped him a quarter for promising not to say a word to Waters, and drew a thirsty grin from the old man.

The saloons on the two-block-long street outnumbered anything else from dry goods stores, milliners, and mercantiles to harness makers and gunsmiths. The various structures ranged from tents behind false fronts to buildings made from such green lumber that in the hot sun's drying process, the boards had already sprung free from the nails and stuck out in bows.

Paint was only for the wealthy, save for the hand-painted business signs that looked like the scrawlings of children in the lower grades of school. A few businesses, hoping to earn respectability and show pride of ownership, hung out billboards made with artistic skill. The Bye Gilly Saloon was one of them. It showed shamrocks in bold green on a field of yellow, and the letters were in bright red.

Slocum sauntered down the boardwalk, which needed repair and was made of such cheese-box-thin lumber it threatened to give way under each footfall. He kept an eye on every step, and soon he pushed in through the deep-green, louvered batwing doors. The place reeked of chewing tobacco, stale cigar smoke, and sour liquor. There was a whang of human and horse sweat as well.

The place was empty save for a few drunks cleaning up. A man with a pencil-sized mustache attached to a thin face, which reminded Slocum of a barn rat, came down the bar to him. "What'll it be, me man?"

"A double shot of decent whiskey."

"Ah, and that'll be four bits for the good stuff."

"There a rancher here named Waters?" Slocum twisted and looked the place over as he dug out the money.

"Ah, I ain't seen Frank in two days. He's long overdue. You might ask Margie up at the Roll On Moose."

"That some French place?"

The man laughed. "Yeah, but no one could spell it so that's how they painted the sign."

Slocum considered the whiskey in the glass. Francie hadn't been wrong about how Waters spent his leisure time in Tascosa. Margie must have him right in her bunk. Slocum sipped the whiskey to wash some of the trail dust out of his throat. He still didn't have a good plan for kicking Waters's ass and sending him home—he'd thought about it riding all the way across the panhandle. Something would come to him.

After downing the glass, he thanked the barman.

"Kin I tell him you was here if'n he comes in?" the man asked.

"Naw, I'd like to surprise him."

"Mum's me word." He sealed his mouth with his finger.

"Thanks."

It was midday and everyone, except for a colored girl dressed in a maid's outfit, was still asleep at the whorehouse. She ushered him inside the dark parlor with the shades drawn.

"Who you be needing?" she asked politely.

"Margie."

She motioned to him and he followed her up the stairs, which creaked under his boot soles. He'd fall through something yet before he left this place. At the door she tried the knob. It clicked open and she smiled. "She ain't got's no one in there or it be locked. You's can go in and wake her up."

He thanked her with a two-bit tip and slipped in to the room. He found Margie lying on her stomach, her honey-brown hair spilled over the pillow. He took a seat in the high-back chair and glanced over at the open trunk. A cartridge belt wrapped around a six-gun in a holster sat atop a blanket in the open chest. He reached over and picked it up. FW was scratched on the butt of the revolver. With quiet stealth, he put it back in place and wondered if it belonged to Frank Waters.

Why would she have one of his guns?

He stepped over and shook her shoulder gently, then settled back in the chair. "Where's Frank?"

"Huh?" She bolted upright, not caring who saw her bare titties, and blinked at him. "I don't know who you mean."

"Frank Waters," he said softly, leaning forward with his elbows on his knees. From her ashen face, she looked too upset to convince him she wasn't lying through her teeth.

"Why, I ain't seen him in a week."

"Think again. You left the Bye Gilly with him night before last, and he ain't been seen since."

"I never—"

"Where did you plant him and where's his money?"

She was shaking her head hard, but she was lying, and he knew that she knew he knew. He reached over and unfurled the gun belt.

"Frank never would have left this behind."

Her face grew paler and she began to tremble, sitting on her heels on the bed as naked as Eve. "I swear—"

"Don't bother. Where's he at?"

"I don't know—I swear—"

"Tell me where he's at."

"Booth'll kill me."

"Booth kill him?"

Her slow nod was enough.

"Where's he buried?"

"In a wash north of town."

"Get your clothes on. You're taking me there. Why did Booth kill him?"

"He said Waters had lots of money. He promised to take me out of here when things cooled off."

"Where's Booth now?"

"I ain't seen him since then."

"Since when?"

"That night he took Waters out of here."

"You figure Booth double-crossed you?"

"Maybe," she said with a snarl, busy buttoning up her dress.

"Let me see. You got Waters drunk, took his gun, and hid it. Then you and Booth took him out the back way to the wash, huh?"

She gave a wooden nod. "Or Booth said he'd kill me."

"Then in the wash, Booth shot him, right?"

"It didn't sound that bad at first. I mean, I thought he was only going to rob him."

"But when Waters sobered up, he'd know you two robbed him."

"Booth said that." She sat on the bed buttoning up her shoes. "He had to do it or he'd get us."

"That the last time you saw Booth?"

"Yeah."

"You beginning to think he ran out on you?"

"Maybe. He took all the money."

"Did he have much?"

"I think so. The money belt was heavy. He never took it off in bed with me, and about squashed me with it each time. He had it full of gold coins. Never paid me one."

So she helped Booth kill Waters and then Booth left her holding the bag. "Come on, I need his body."

"What for?"

"To give him a decent burial."

"He don't deserve it He treated me like I was a bitch dog."

"Yeah. Well, he may have deserved it, but that ain't no reason to murder him for his damn money."

She looked at Slocum with a mean eye. "He rubbed my belly clear raw with that canvas money belt to show me who he was."

"Killing a man who mistreated you is one thing. But robbing him for his money is a crime even in this hellhole. Move out. I'm buying a shovel at the store to dig him up."

"Oh, Jesus, I have to see him again?"

"I didn't put him there. Now move."

She gave him a disdainful look and mumbled about what Waters did to her.

He bought a shovel for a dollar, and came out and told her to lead the way. In front of the undertaker's, he told her to stop and stuck his head inside. "You have a coffin for a large man?"

The bald man looked up from his work on one. "Who would that be, pray tell, my good man?"

"Frank Waters."

"Aye, and he'd need a big one. You on your way to kill him?"

"No, he was shot and robbed two days ago. I'm going to exhume his body."

"And who would be the party done that?"

"A man named Booth, and she's showing me where Waters is at." He nodded toward Margie, who was standing with her hand on her hip, an impatient look on her face.

"I be getting the marshal. I'll be right after you."

"Fine," Slocum said, and indicated Margie should move on.

"Suppose they'll hang me?" she asked in a quiet voice as she lifted her skirts to keep up with him.

"I think they'll give you a horse and tell you to never show up again."

"Why?"

"You know too much about their sex lives to speak out from the gallows about either the size of their dicks or letting their wives know how they frequented the Moose house."

"I do, don't I?"

"Exactly."

They dropped off the road into the sandy wash. When he saw her fighting to walk in the loose fill, he offered his hand, but she refused. "It ain't far. Booth just put him at the base and loosened the dirt so it collapsed over him."

"I've done that before in the case of an emergency."

"When he shot him—chills ran through my body. I never killed no one in my life. I'd a liked to killed some. That preacher stole my cherry when I was thirteen. Farris Fenton—I'd a killed him. Frank, he rubbed me raw but I'd

a never killed him for that. I'd a killed them Barley brothers that raped me the week after the preacher popped it. I
think he—" She stopped and huffed for breath. Then she
pointed. "It's right up there. See the cave-in?"

He did and went to work. He pitched a few scoops aside
and found the man's boot. Wonder the varmints hadn't dug
him up already. By the time the townfolks arrived, he had
him uncovered. Frank Waters had a swarthy complexion
with a full beard floured in tan Texas soil. He was a barrel-
chested man. In his dirt coating, he only looked half as im-
pressive as he must have alive. The undertaker and two
others lowered him in to the coffin.

"It's Frank, all right," the funeral man announced.

A murmur from the crowd at his words sounded like a
groan. Slocum wondered if they'd really miss Waters from
what he'd heard and knew about. Still, murder shocked
even the residents of the toughest place he knew of this
side of hell.

The man with the marshal star cleared his throat. "How
did you know to find him here?"

"Let's say a bird told me. We need to talk over there."
Slocum nodded toward the other side of the wash.

The lawman told the others he'd tell them more later
and to go back to their own businesses. Margie flounced
down on the ground and hugged her knees. A few of the
onlookers got an eyeful before she discovered they could
see her bare butt and dropped her legs down. She wrinkled
her nose at them for peeking.

"What's she got to do with it?" the lawman asked.

"Let's say she had privileged information. I told her she
could have a horse and get the hell out of here for helping
me find him. You go along with that?"

"We might not ever have found him. Who—" He lowered his voice. "Did this?"

"A fella named Booth robbed him and shot him in the
back of the head. Two days ago."

"What's your part in it?"

"Waters's wife was concerned about him and asked me to check on him when I was here."

"I never caught your name."

"Tom White." They shook hands.

"Max Snyder's mine. Well, Tom White, I sure thank you. I'll get a murder warrant out for Booth. No telling where he is at."

"No telling. I'll pay for Waters's burial. His place is four hard days by wagon from here."

"He's near ripe now." Then Snyder nodded toward Margie. "Will you get her out of town tonight?"

"She'll be gone."

"Might send her on the stage."

"Either way, I'll have her gone."

Marshal Snyder stalked away to two onlookers down the wash. The three soon went back to the road and disappeared.

"What now?" Margie asked. Her dress up, knees apart and exposing the black thatch at the base of her wrinkled flat stomach, she idly tossed small stones at the wash.

"I got you a pardon if you leave town tonight."

"Aw, damn, I guess I owe you." She took his hand and he pulled her to her feet.

"No, just stay away from the Booths of this world."

She laughed aloud. "Who do you think comes and fucks a whore anyway? Ain't many saints get hard-ons."

"That's your problem."

"My problem's I'm twenty-four. In another few years, a pig ranch will be all there is left for me. Them cute little gals in their teens get the good jobs in them plush parlors. After that, you come work in rat holes like Tascosa. When they're through with you here, you can go and screw them black buffalo soldiers at the pig ranches. Ain't much future for me when I leave here, is there?"

"Beats hanging."

She looked around the wash and shook her head. "Just takes longer."

"Find you a job cooking for an outfit. They hire women. No telling you might find a real man out there."

"Aw, hell, I got the mark like Cain on my forehead." She paused at the top of the climb to catch her breath. "Once a whore, always one."

"You can choose that, not me. I'll have a horse out back of the Moose at midnight. Take him or leave him."

"I better not go back there. There will be too many questions. The livery man will hide me until dark for a big favor." She wrinkled her nose at the prospect.

"Good, that's even better. Take Waters's saddle horse and rig after dark and get clear of this place. Here's forty bucks to tide you over." He handed her the paper money.

On an impulse, she kissed him and hugged his neck. Her lilac perfume filled his nostrils. "Gawdamn, you're a helluva nice man and I ain't ever even turned a trick with you."

"Just stay out of sight and get gone."

"I will. You ever want a real piece of ass, you look me up. Hear me?"

He nodded, and went on with the shovel on his shoulder. Where had Booth gone?

19

He stopped in the Bye Gilly Saloon, spoke to the bartender, and ordered a double. The man poured it in the glass.

"Heard yah found Waters dead."

"Yeah, a bullet in the brain usually ends in death, especially at close range."

"Why was he killed?"

"Money, Waters must have carried a large sum on him."

"Ah, in a waist wallet, huh? I remember some dumb bloke breaking his fist hitting him in the gut during a fight. Said it was like steel."

Slocum nodded and tossed down some of the whiskey. He needed to do several things—find Booth first and recover the money for Francie, then hire some cowboys, load a wagon with supplies, and get back to her place. "Any idea where Booth might be?"

The bartender leaned over and whispered, "See that tall drink of water looking over the card game back there. One Eye is what they call him. He's a friend of Booth's."

Slocum nodded, downed his whiskey, and thanked him. He set the glass on the bar, walked over to stand near the man, then scratched a match as if to light an imaginary cigar and drew his attention. One Eye glanced over with his good eye, and Slocum nodded toward an empty table.

A patch covered One Eye's sunken socket. He dropped in to a chair at the table opposite the chair Slocum chose. In a soft voice, Slocum began. "I need to know where Booth is."

"How should I know?" One Eye shrugged his narrow shoulders under the wash-worn collarless shirt.

"Oh, you know, and I'm willing to pay you forty dollars for that information." Slocum sat back, tented his fingers, and touched his nose. "That's two months wages for no work. What's Booth paying yah?"

One Eye looked around as if to check if they'd attracted any attention. Then, looking satisfied, he turned back to Slocum. "Let's see the color of your money."

Slocum took out a small roll and peeled off two twenties. As One Eye looked on shocked, Slocum tore the bills in half and tossed two halves on the table. "You get the rest when I get Booth," Slocum said.

"I never—"

"Listen, you're one eye away from being blind. You cross me and you'll be feeling your way around in the permanent dark." Slocum's eyes narrowed to underscore the threat.

"All right. All right. He's got a homesteader outfit about ten miles north of here."

From his vest pockets, Slocum drew a stub of a pencil and a small piece of paper. "Make me a map."

One Eye shook his head. "I ain't no artist."

"Draw it."

"You take the road to Kansas up to Snake Crick. It'll be dry. You can't miss it. There's a broken-down wagon half buried in the sand. Go down that wash for a mile. The cabin is on the right. It ain't much. Said the settler was killed trying to save a baby that was washed away in a flood."

"You'll get your other half when I get Booth."

"What if he kills you?"

"Then get it from him." Slocum left the man's company. On his way out, he slapped a silver dollar on the bar for the barkeep and nodded in approval at him.

Max Snyder looked up from his paperwork when Slocum walked in to his small office. "You know anything else, White?"

"Booth's up on Snake Creek in an abandoned shack."

Snyder wiped his mouth with his palm. "Holy crap, you don't waste any time finding things out, do you?"

"You want to ride up there with me? I want the money he took for Waters's widow, Frances."

As if he was thinking about it, Snyder nodded his head slowly. "She's a lucky woman that she's got you for a friend. The chances of her getting that money back would have been nil if you hadn't lended a hand in this business."

"I just want justice done. Besides, Booth had a good friend of mine gunned down."

"I see. Deputy U.S. Marshal Hooker is over at the Moose. He'll want to go along too."

"Get him. Booth ever learns about us finding the Waters body and he'll run."

"He's damn sure liable to. Meet you at the livery in ten minutes." Snyder grabbed his hat and rushed out.

Slocum closed the office door when he left. He bought some jerky for the trip in the mercantile and when he came out of the store, he saw the two lawmen. The big man was putting on his suit coat as he came on the run down the empty street with Snyder.

Hooker was a rotund man with a white walrus mustache. His blue eyes were cold as ice and the mustache hid his mouth except when he spoke. "Snyder says you've got this killer spotted."

Slocum nodded. "He's supposed to be in a shack on Snake Creek."

"Good, Let's ride then. How far?"

"Ten miles or so up on Snake Creek."

"You know the place?" Hooker asked Snyder.

"I've been up there. Not this place, but I know where it's at."

"Daylight's burning," Hooker said. "We better ride."

The three saddled up and rode out down the main street.

"Where yah headed?" somebody shouted from a store porch at Snyder.

"To Kansas to find a bootlegger."

"Hell, there's plenty of them around here." His words drew some laughter and a scowl from the marshal. They pushed on at a trot.

The sun was setting in a rosy cloud formation when they reached Snake Creek. They'd have an hour of twilight to locate Booth. The three dismounted close by the half-buried wagon box and broken spokes. Looking in different directions, they began to piss. The streams arced out until their bladders were empty.

"Snyder interrupt anything?" Slocum asked the marshal with a grin. "Getting you out of the Moose?"

"Naw, I'd had my toss in the hay. They asked me if I knew where what's-her-name went. I didn't know shit about her."

"Margie?"

"Yeah."

"She's leaving. I've got her stashed till the evening stage comes." Slocum said to cover her tracks.

Hooker nodded and they mounted up, following some horseshoe prints in the loose fill that had been washed in during the last flood. The long shadows of twilight had begun to creep in to the dry creek bed. They dismounted, thinking they were close to Booth, and picketed their horses. Hooker took a Winchester out of his scabbard and they set out on foot. Rounding a bend, Slocum smelled a whiff of smoke and stopped them.

They nodded at each other. They were close. As they edged around the sheer bank, guns in hand, Slocum caught sight of the shack and a light in a small window. They split up, and Snyder went west to the cover of some brush. Hooker went to the side, and Slocum, moving low, approached from the front.

Gun in his fist, Slocum recalled the sight of Don Jeminez's stiff body pinned down by the dead mule Tonto on the hillside. *Make one mistake, Booth, and you'll be roasting your nuts in hell.* He was fifty feet away from the cabin in the growing darkness. He dropped to one knee, knowing that the others should be in place.

"Booth! Booth! Throw your gun out and come out with your hands high or die."

"Go to hell, you sumbitch."

Hooker answered with two swift bullets that shattered a row of jars in the window and doused the light inside.

Coughing and choking, Booth shouted that he was giving up.

"One trick and you're dead," Slocum said as he moved in toward the bent-over figure coughing up his guts as he came outside.

"Where's Waters's money?" He jerked Booth upright.

"What money?"

Slocum slashed him across the face with his pistol barrel. "Where is it?"

He held his arm up in self-defense. "Damn you! It's in there on the table."

"Handcuff him," Slocum said to Snyder and stalked over to the doorway. He struck a match and located a candle on the table. He lit the wick and spotted the canvas belt. It looked intact. He checked a few of the pouches and nodded to Hooker, who was standing in the doorway. "Guess it's all here."

"How much, you reckon?"

"Guess we can count it."

"Naw, let's make some food. Best part is that we got him and the money."

Slocum nodded. "Best thing, yes."

They ate some bacon and fried potatoes out of Booth's meager larder and, with him chained to a tree, slept a few hours. Before sunup, they saddled his horse and took him to Tascosa.

In town, Slocum gave them each a hundred-dollar reward from the wallet. They shook his hand and acted grateful. Snyder put Booth in a cell, and Slocum had the belt locked in the mercantile safe until he was ready to leave for the ranch.

By that afternoon, he'd hired three cowboys for Francie. Buck, a blue-eyed, freckle-faced puncher in his twenties who could rope anything including a pig, showed Slocum his skill on a loose shoat in the street. Rake, the youngest, hardly out of his teens, was eager for work—Slocum found him at the livery swamping out the stalls. The oldest, Teodoro, was Mexican and could make a reata sing. He wore a high-crowned sombrero and carried a fiddle he could play.

"Who has a horse of his own?" Slocum asked his new crew in front of the livery.

"I do," Buck said.

"I have my own, Señor," said the Mexican.

Slocum nodded to the kid. "You get to drive the wagon. You got any tack?"

"No, sir."

"I'll find you a saddle and some spurs. We all had to learn how." Slocum dropped his gaze to the ground. "Any man here can't take orders from a woman better stay here."

"Couple of square meals a day and twenty-five a month and I'd be happy working for anyone," Buck said. "Bet her cooking would beat most ranch cooks anyway."

"No problem for me, Señor."

"No, sir," the kid said. "I'm just proud to get a chance."

"There's lots of work out there. Waters spent more time here than tending his business."

"When we leave?" Buck asked.

"In the morning. They're loading the supplies this afternoon."

"You need us to oversee that?" Buck asked.

"Wouldn't be a bad idea. Hitch up the wagon and take it down there. Pick the kid out a saddle, slicker, and spurs too. I missed anything you can think of, put them on the list."

"Thanks," the youth said to Slocum as he grinned.

Slocum crossed the street looking for One Eye in Gilly's. From the swinging doors, he asked the bartender about him.

"I ain't seen him today, Tom. But I heard yah brought in that killer."

"He's in the jail."

"Good. Next whiskey is on me."

"Thanks. See him, tell him I got his money."

"I will."

There were three thousand and fifty dollars in gold coins in that belt. Was that from cattle sales or what? That much money in one man's wallet looked strange. Slocum would probably never know the answer, but Francie could damn well ranch as long as she wanted. He smiled crossing over to the Longhorn Bar across the street as he remembered how Margie had gotten sore from Waters's belt.

He pushed in the batwing doors. "One Eye in here?"

The barkeep shook his head and threw a rag over his shoulder. "Not today."

"Thanks."

He saw the boys hitching the team up at the livery. He went to the jail and stuck his head inside the door. "How's things going?"

"I'm taking Booth to the fort in the morning."

"Be a good idea."

"Army's got a better jail."

Slocum nodded and went down to the mercantile. Buck had the list and stood with a young clerk out front. Buck was telling the young man in the white apron how he wanted the items placed. The boy was listening good. There was a good used saddle on the hitch rack, and when the kid came out he nodded toward the rig.

"Got spurs and a slicker too, boss."

"Good. Teodoro, you got any extra strings for that fiddle?" he asked the man.

"No, Señor."

"Get some and put them on the ranch's bill. The boss lady loves that music."

"Ah, *sí*. I am in love with her already."

"She put up with that cranky Waters for a long time. She needs some spoiling." Slocum stopped the fresh-faced clerk. "Got any flower seeds?"

"Yes, sir."

"Put some in the order."

"But it's late—"

"She can dream all winter about planting them next year. You ever wait on Waters when he loaded up?"

"I-I did."

"What did he take back?"

"I'd say bare essentials."

"I thought so. Add in dried apples, raisins, airtight cases—four peaches and six tomatoes, brown sugar, sorghum lick, cinnamon, vanilla."

"He never ordered any of them except a few cans for himself—to eat going home, I figured."

"One more thing," Slocum stopped the boy. "He always paid cash?"

"Yes, sir."

"That's fine, go ahead. I just wondered." It cost Waters plenty to chase whores and drink, play poker—where in hell did it come from? Maybe Slocum would never know.

Rake reined up the team as Slocum and the others approached. "What's happened?"

"Booth escaped," Buck said.

The kid stood up, holding the lines tight, and looked around the top of the tarp at their back trail. "He coming after us?"

"Sleep with your six-gun is all I kin say." Buck dismounted and joined the others getting a drink from the water barrel on the side of the rig.

"I ain't got one," said Rake.

"Gawdamn, boy, we took you to raise, I guess."

"Don't worry, you'll have one," Slocum said and frowned at Buck. "Did you go to Kansas as a swamper for Cookie the first time?"

Buck stopped the dipper gourd short of his face. "Yes, sir."

"Then remember that trip. Rake ain't doing half bad."

Buck nodded and finished his drink. "I will."

"Good."

The fourth day they reached the ranch, and Francie rode out on a bay horse to meet them. One troubled look at each of them and she frowned. "Where's he at?"

"Frank's dead," Slocum said. "I had him buried there. He was shot in a robbery scheme." He waved the boys on. "We'll be there in a short while."

They all had their hats off for her, and they rode on with a pleased nod.

She dismounted and ran over to hug Slocum. "Oh, I'm so glad you found him. How much do I owe for the goods?"

He squeezed her. "Frank ever say he had money from the cattle?"

"No. He said they never paid the bills and he owed for the past year's supplies. So we were real careful what we got and laid off the hands soon as we could because things were so bad."

"Frank ever been an outlaw?"

"Why ask me that?" She shook her head as if that was impossible.

"Well, he didn't owe a soul in Tascosa. He paid cash for everything he got in the past, and all I can find is he was stingy about the supplies he brought out here."

She blinked her eyes at him.

"I recovered over three thousand dollars from the murdering thief in a money belt he stole off Frank."

"Three—" She sucked in her breath and he caught her as she fainted.

When her eyelids fluttered, he smiled down at her. "I want to search the ranch. I think your husband had more money from some source other than cattle."

"But where?"

He shook his head and eased her onto her feet. "We may never find the rest." He showed her a gold twenty-dollar piece that glinted in the sun. "Fresh-minted."

"But—"

He caught the horses and started for the distant house.

"Thought you couldn't come back," she said, looking at the dusty toes of her scuffed boots peeking from under the hem of her dress as she walked.

"I had to. Besides, if there is more, maybe we can find it."

She stepped in front of him. Her arms shot around his neck and she closed her eyes for him to kiss her. When they parted, she stood flush-faced in his way. "And I worried it was Frank coming back and he'd have more bad news. That bastard."

So they made wild love at night in her bed and used the days to search. The hands rode out each day at daybreak to make a tally book of the FW cattle that Buck kept. At night they came in, dropping heavy out of the saddle, each day picking up more of the remuda horses in their journeys.

On Saturday night, she told them to rest on Sunday, and they smiled in appreciation. "I can stay in the house and you all can take a bath in the tank if you warn me."

"We will, ma'am," Buck said with his hat wadded in his hand.

After supper, when the boys had gone to the bunkhouse, she told Slocum Buck would make a good foreman, and he agreed. He climbed on a chair and used his knife on a loose rock he'd noticed in the upper chimney structure.

"Find anything?"

"Bring a light." He reached inside and found a yellow newspaper and unfurled it. The headline said: JESSE ROBS THE TRAIN. He stepped down and began to read aloud.

In broad daylight seven members of the James Gang had struck the mail car on a Missouri Pacific train and taken the army payroll worth over thirty thousand dollars. The murderous outlaws had struck while the train was being watered at a small station and water tower called Erp some sixty miles southwest of Saint Louis. They commandeered the crew and then ordered the mail car opened. After a brief shoot-out leaving two of the four soldier guards wounded, they took the payroll and loaded it in a wagon, a conveyance that they had stolen earlier in the day along with its two powerful mules. They shot the car ceilings full of holes, making the passengers take cover on the floor, and thankfully, except for a few who were nicked by stray bullets, all were unhurt.

Various posses took up the trail, but no doubt the bandits were hidden by Confederate sympathizers in the region, for no trace was found of them. Seven men on fancy-grade horses, all strangers to the land, driving a stolen team and wagon, and they'd all disappeared.

According to the article, Pinkerton agents were still searching the region for any witnesses and gang members. Anyone with any information about this robbery or the James gang should contact Pinkerton Detective Agency. Post Office Box 34, Saint Louis, Missouri. Generous rewards were offered for any information.

"Did it say what color those mules were?"

Slocum looked up and shook his head. "Why?"

She looked at the date of the robbery. "He showed up in McDonald County shortly after that date and bought a farm right next to ours."

"He ever wear a canvas wallet around you?"

"No."

"He did in Tascosa."

"Any money up there?" She nodded toward the chimney.

He stood up on the chair, reached in, and found two more sacks. The canvas was almost rotten as he eased the sacks down to Francie. She set them on the table and sighed. "How much are they worth?"

"A thousand apiece, I figure."

"Wow, I can build a ranch, can't I?"

He hugged her and swung her around until she threw her head back. "Did he steal that money from the gang?"

"He might have. Guess we'll never know."

She snuggled to his chest. "All those years he hid the whole thing from me and we lived like paupers."

Holding her tight, he rocked her back and forth.

The door burst open and Slocum stared at the gun in Booth's hand. "Move a muscle and you're both dead." One Eye slipped in the door.

"Where did you get this newspaper?" Booth picked it up. "James Gang," he scoffed. "They was looking for Jesse all right. Wasn't them at all. Big Frank switched the money to his own wagon and they killed them damn stolen mules and buried them and the wagon. No way they'd find us. They was looking for Jesse and the other Frank." Booth laughed and nodded to One Eye,

"You recognize him in Tascosa?" Slocum asked.

"Yeah, I recognized him before that. But when that whore Margie said he wore a hole in her belly with his heavy wallet, I figured he still had part of the loot."

"He didn't remember you?"

"Naw, I was the kid stole the first wagon and mules for

John Keyes. Keyes paid me. Waters never knew me. Then later I learned one of the gang got off with all the money. Keyes let it slip one day that his name was Waters. Boy, he'd've given me a big reward for this." Booth slammed the sack down and the coins spilled out on the floor.

Both Booth and One Eye dived for the money. Then the room exploded in shots. The sulfurous gun smoke made Slocum and Francie cough and stagger outside.

"You all right, ma'am?" Buck asked her. "Sorry, but we didn't want you or Slocum shot, so Teo and I waited until they got distracted."

"You two did good." Slocum clapped the short Mexican on the shoulder. "Saved our skins."

Francie nodded. "Yes, thank you."

They buried the dead men at sunup and took the day off.

21

The following March, Slocum was on the road to Mexico south of San Antonio. Short new cheatgrass had begun to wave in the spring wind. A week earlier, he'd read in the *San Antonio Clarion* where bounty hunter Wesley Harrigan had been killed in a shoot-out with two outlaws near Mason, Texas. He'd left the information about Belle Nelson's bank account with her bereaved parents when he had been through their place in north Texas. As far as he was concerned, he had the whole thing wound up.

The trail drovers had begun to stir with long lines of cattle streaming across the Rio Grande. Two thousand head to the outfit, they lined out in mile-long ribbons of horn-clacking three-and four-year-old steers. Their cloven hooves cut the tender new shoots of wildflowers intending to spread their seed over this land after they blossomed (if they survived). Riders, hoarse from yelling, cracked whips and waved coils of rope at their wards, which made a constant bawl of complaint about how they wanted to bolt back to the thorny thickets rather than make the trek northward.

"You going to stand there the whole day and block the damn road, mister?"

Something familiar in that voice made him look hard at the woman on the seat with a handful of leather reins and wearing a wide-brimmed man's hat, collarless shirt, galluses over her breasts, and new canvas pants. A Colt with a redwood-handle stuck out of a holster on her side. With her dusty boot planted on the dash, she smiled.

"It's me. Margie."

"You the cook for this outfit?"

She winked at him. "And a damn good one. This bunch would fight you if you messed with me."

Slocum rode up close holding his hands up. "I don't doubt it. You like it?"

"Beats the hell out of bedding every sorry sumbitch comes through the damn door and having to like it." She wiped her nose on her sleeve, holding the mules in check. "I sure don't miss it."

Slocum winked at her. "You still owe me."

"I'll pay you back too—someday. But I better get my butt up there and make camp for tonight. Get up there, Jud. Judy! Get your fanny over." She clucked to them and blew him a kiss.

Santa Maria was the sleepy town across the Rio Bravo where the music was sweeter and the women prettier. He twisted in the saddle and watched the rocking canvas top of the Bar K chuck wagon. Margie was driving her mules toward the old North Star. No pig ranch for that girl.

He set the dun horse in a lope—Santa Maria called him.

Watch for

SLOCUM'S REVENGE TRAIL

346th novel in the exciting SLOCUM series
from Jove

Coming in December!